Single to Peking

Single to Peking

By Val Broom

BROWN
DOG
BOOKS

Published under licence by Brown Dog Books and
The Self-Publishing Partnership, 7 Green Park Station, Bath BA1 1JB

www.selfpublishingpartnership.co.uk

ISBN printed book: 978-1-78545-067-9
ISBN e-book: 978-1-78545-068-6

Cover design by Kevin Rylands

Printed and bound by CPI Group (UK) Ltd, Croydon CR0 4YY

For dear Graham,
with love and thanks for your
unfailing encouragement and all
that word processing.

Chapter 1

The wagons of the Trans-Siberian train shuddered, lurched and ground to a halt yet again. Helena had not really been asleep, but the sudden change in motion roused her and she gently snuggled little Erica to her, soothing the child while she wondered for perhaps the hundredth time why she had agreed to do this epic journey across foreign lands, by herself except for her feisty little three-year-old.

Back in Berlin, five years ago, Helena's life in the Pension of her adopted parents had been rather mundane but safe and happy. After leaving school she had hoped to take a secretarial course and work in an office like the glamorous young women who frequented the smart shops in Unter den Linden, but unfortunately her Mama had been taken ill and developed pleurisy so Helena was needed to help with the cleaning and cooking for the lodgers. Even after her recovery Helena's mother did not seem robust so the secretarial course never happened.

Most of the lodgers in the Pension were students at the nearby university who stayed a short time and brought a lively presence to the old house. Sometimes Helena would be invited to accompany them to college socials or the vibrant café scene, where groups of young people talked politics or art and often sang rousing songs.

Looking back, the day life really changed was the day Fu Yan came to stay at the Pension. He was older than most of the student guests, having been seconded to German universities as part of an academic exchange programme between the German and Chinese governments. He was very fastidious and insisted on the best room in the house, willingly paying extra to receive it. In spite of some language barriers his charm soon melted their reservations and his natural charisma and impeccable manners endeared him to them.

Socialising with the family helped Fu Yan to improve his German and he soon found he was enjoying Helena's company very much. Soon they were spending most of their free time together. They strolled along the banks of the River Spree, visited the famous zoo and went to Tea Dances in the Hotel Aldon, the most expensive and opulent hotel in Berlin – how different this all was from the poor students who usually stayed at the Pension!

Some month's later part of Fu Yan's studies meant he had to work at Heidelberg University for two or three semesters. The family were saddened by this news, both for the loss of the income and his friendship. Farewells were said and at the last moment Helena accompanied him to the railway station. With only moments to spare before the train left Fu Yan leant towards Helena and kissed her lips with such sensuous passion that she was left bewildered and quite shocked. Then tears welled in her eyes at the thought that she may never see him again.

The very next morning an urgent knock at the door revealed a telegram boy. Telegrams always gave Frau Weber, Helena's Mama, a shock and with a thumping heart she opened it to read

"Back at the weekend. Keep room. Fu Yan."

Fu Yan had realised he was in love with Helena and could not be parted from her. For all his time in Heidelberg he travelled to that city for the week and returned at the weekends. When he left each Sunday to return to his studies, Frau Weber always gave him bread and wurst for the trip but he confessed to Helena that he always threw it out of the train window because in his words, "only peasants eat packed food on trains".

By Christmas Fu Yan was almost one of the family and was enchanted by the colourful German traditions of a family Christmas. He entered into the spirit of the celebration and appeared at the traditional Christmas Eve dinner in a stunning evening suit that enhanced his dark good looks. One of the first things Helena had noticed about him was how well his expensive European clothes suited him and how handsome he looked, not at all what she and her younger (also adopted) sister had expected when they heard a Chinese man was to be one of their guests.

The train creaked and rumbled as it started up again bringing Helena back to the chilly and uncomfortable present in the carriage winding its way through the vast forests and mountainous landscape of Mongolia. Little Erica stirred, whimpered and asked for a drink. The only way to obtain a warm drink was to go to the samovar at the end of each carriage. Hoping it would have been well-tended during the night, Helena left Erica for a moment and went to get tea.

When she returned she discovered the reason for the latest stop in the shapes of some rough-looking Russian soldiers who were now taking up most of the carriage. They looked bone weary and made no comment as she squeezed through and clasped her daughter to her. Helena was to get no more sleep that night and determined to see the guard first thing to complain about this invasion of privacy.

In the morning the guard was nowhere to be found and due to the arrival of the soldiers there was no more food available until the next stop. Helena searched through one of her smaller cases and found the last of the German biscuits for little Erica and then tried to distract her with a new drawing game. Such a long journey had been boring for the child but she was in general happy, contented and very amenable as long as she got her own way.

The soldiers in the carriage were frequently swigging from bottles of vodka, of which they seem to have an inexhaustible supply, and Helena was glad when they wandered off to join some comrades who were singing rousing traditional songs further down the train. Just one Cossack remained snoring loudly in the corner. After a time, however, he awoke and began watching Helena and Erica at their game.

Soon he moved closer and Helena began to feel uncomfortable, with good reason, as he suddenly sprang forward and tried to kiss her. She screamed and kicked against his legs as hard as she could, thinking only to protect her child from danger. Thankfully a moment later a sharp order rang out and a young Russian captain called the man to attention and rapidly dismissed him.

Helena was mightily relieved and thanked her saviour while trying to straighten her clothes and comfort Erica.

"Captain Petrovsky at your service Fraulein," the tall elegant Russian clicked his heels and did a mock salute.

"How did you know I was German?".

"I heard you talking to your little girl. She is very pretty. Are you travelling alone with her?"

Helena was a little unsure of his motives so she said, "Oh, we are meeting some friends at the next station."

"May I remain here until then?"

"Of course."

The next station proved to be a good many miles away and for all that time the captain chatted amiably and behaved impeccably. He talked about happy times in his youth spent with friends in Germany on walking holidays, which was where he picked up his knowledge of the language. When no friends appeared at the station he made no comment but Helena began to feel uncomfortable that she had lied to such a charming man.

When he asked directly how far she was travelling, Helena thought she must explain her situation – that she was travelling to Peking to join her husband. She found herself also explaining how they had met and married in Berlin and how Fu Yan had promised to send for her very soon but she had not seen him for more than three years.

"So your husband has not seen his little daughter?"

"No indeed, and –"suddenly all Helena's anxiety about the journey and uncertainty about the new life she was heading towards flooded into her mind and she was unable to hold back the tears of fear.

What if she didn't love Fu Yan anymore?

What if he didn't love her?

Would Erica learn to love her Papa?

How would she cope with life in a strange land with very different customs and a totally unintelligible and unpronounceable language?

More immediately Helena knew she soon would have to change trains and had no idea how she would manage to cope with all her luggage and Erica, never mind finding the right train or buying her ticket.

Captain Petrovsky waited a few minutes and then hesitantly tried to offer a few words of comfort. Helena quickly required her composure, feeling most embarrassed and apologised.

"My dear lady, no need to apologise, but can I be of assistance?"

"I know we have to change to the Trans-Manchurian Line at Harbin and I would be grateful for some help with all my luggage if possible."

"Of course! I will gladly arrange for some of the men to help you, Madam."

Helena thanked him sincerely and the next few hours were passed in occasional polite conversation.

At Harbin, where the train drew in late into the afternoon, Captain Petrovsky called two corporals and arranged for the luggage to be transferred to the platform, privately watching in amazement that one young woman and child could need so much luggage.

It was now necessary to find out about the train and here matters became worse. It seemed that the next train to Peking was in two days' time. Helena had expected to have to wait but not that long!

"I have but a short time Madam," said Captain Petrovsky. "Once the train is refuelled and provisioned I must re-join my men to continue to the front. May I be of any further assistance before I leave?"

"Oh, I understand, Captain, you have been so helpful already. We are very grateful to you."

Helena did not want to impose by asking for any further help but looking around at the bustling scene she had no idea how to find a place to stay for herself and Erica. Captain Petrovsky seemed to read her thoughts for his next words were, "Would you like me to try to find a Hostel or Pension for you?"

"Oh, yes please, but could we first send a telegram to my husband in Peking?"

The telegraph office was nearby and Helena carefully printed out a message:

"Zug aus Harbin u"bermorgen" ("Train leaves Harbin day after tomorrow," – economical German words are sometimes very practical!)

Harbin seemed a frantically busy town; all the streets blocked with a mixture of military and agricultural traffic while the people of the town tried to go about their daily business. Captain Petrovsky knew the only way to find a room would be to 'grease a palm', as the saying goes, and, telling Helena to wait for him, he plunged into the melee of the street to find a likely candidate.

Quite soon he returned and led Helena and Erica to a grimy foreboding house around the corner.

"I am sorry this is the best I can find as you need to be near the station. I must leave now but I will secure your luggage with the guard and wish you Bon Voyage and a good new life." He turned to go with a polite bow but then immediately turned back. Reaching into his tunic he withdrew a small revolver and held it towards Helena. "Take this, dear lady, for your protection." He thrust the gun into her hands and was gone.

The nights on the train had been bad enough but in no way compared to this! The bed was simply a stone shelf in a large dimly lit room, very much like a dormitory in a workhouse, thought Helena. She tried to make some sort of bed for herself and Erica from some old bits of sacking but she hardly slept a wink, keeping the revolver close on the floor and listening to constant ominous rustling and creaking.

In the morning she discovered that the only sanitation was a tap outside and a hole in the ground, but gritting her teeth she did her best to tidy herself and the child. During the night some other 'guests' had arrived and among them was a young Chinese woman with a little boy about six or seven years old. In the way of children he and Erica regarded each other for a few minutes and then rapidly struck up a rapport, chiefly inspired by the fact that he had collected several cockroaches under the bedding and was attempting to race them against each other.

Helena had been wondering all night how she was going to find somewhere to buy food so she seized the opportunity to smile and greet the boy's mother. By sign language alone she asked the young woman about breakfast, handing her some of the roubles she still had and hoping she could trust her. The young Chinese eagerly grasped the money, which was probably far more than needed, and disappeared into the street leaving the children at their game. Although she was gone some time Helena reasoned that she would be back since she had left her son in the room.

Eventually she returned with some food in curious lidded containers. There was broth with some vegetables floating around, goats' milk for the children and clear scented tea. Helena showed her gratitude, realising that this woman's help could be invaluable for these two difficult days.

The air in the hostel was dank and musty, adding to the general atmosphere of dismal deprivation. Helena determined to take Erica out for some fresh air, even though she felt nervous about venturing into the town and certainly she would not go far for fear of getting lost. Holding the child's hand tightly and with her handbag firmly grasped in the other hand, she ventured out directly onto a grimy unmade path. Just a few steps led them to the railway station area and they were immediately enveloped in the noise and chaos of the main street.

Having come from the elegance of Berlin, Helena was dismayed by the roughness of the area and, seemingly, the people. Street vendors were clamouring to sell their wares, much of which was unrecognisable to Helena, and ragged children were scavenging around the stalls. There were some Europeans around but all seemed busily intent on their own business. Unable to read any of the signs on shops or buildings, Helena simply walked straight down on one side of the street and back again, avoiding dirt and detritus along the way as much as possible. If young children scavenging horrified her, even more upsetting was the sight of beggars with dead eyes of hopelessness. She was actually glad to regain the hostel and exchange a greeting of sorts with the young Chinese woman.

Wan Mei (they had managed to exchange names) did not leave the hostel at all during the day but sat on the floor watching the children and attempting to repair a large tear in her padded jacket. Whenever anybody passed by she looked up with, Helena felt, fear in her eyes.

The second night was worse than the first now that Helena knew there were cockroaches and strongly suspected rats as well. As they tried to settle down again to sleep she said a little prayer for help and protection in this alien place.

In the morning the young Chinese woman and her son had gone without trace and Helena briefly wondered if they were safe, but soon had to concentrate on the business of catching that train!

The station master had loaded the luggage as arranged, much to Helena's delight, but she noted that one piece was missing and hoped it was not the valise that contained the German sausages and rye bread that Fu Yan had asked her to bring. He had become fond of some aspects of German cuisine during his student years in Germany.

The train was absolutely packed, of course, being one of only two trains per week to Peking, but in First Class they did at least have seats and some room. As soon as the train moved off Erica asked if they were now going back to see her Oma and Opa and Helena found it hard to remain cheerful as she said, "No, we won't see them again for a while."

The child's innocent question triggered an overwhelming feeling of homesickness.

Chapter 2

It was becoming more and more difficult to keep Erica amused and cheerful, understandably since both were so tired and the journey seemed endless. When Erica slept or amused herself for a short time, Helena began to feel more and more alone and anxious.

Gradually the largely desolate countryside gave way to occasional villages where crops of wheat and sweet potatoes grew in small fields. Then came the outskirts of Peking. No city looks attractive when you enter it by rail and Peking was no exception: the small squat shapeless buildings looked shabby and depressing, adding to Helena's desolate frame of mind. The butterflies in her tummy became a swarm of locusts and she had to fight to keep smiling for Erica.

Others in the carriage began to raise themselves and collect up luggage so she guessed their arrival was imminent. She buttoned Erica's coat and quickly combed her thick black hair. For herself Helena tried to smooth her pearl grey costume that had looked so elegant when she had left but was now undeniably crumpled.

With a screech of brakes the train slowed and ponderously nosed into the station. On the platform there were hordes of people, most of them waving excitedly, but it was impossible to pick out the face she was searching for. Taking a deep breath she held Erica's hand and stepped out of the carriage to disembark. The steps of the train were steep and she had to almost jump off and turn to lift Erica down.

As she turned back to face the station the small group of chattering people nearest seemed to part and her gaze fell upon Fu Yan pushing his way through towards her. As their eyes met he stopped and a delighted smile spread across his face, mirrored by Helena's own expression. In that moments the fears and anxieties of the last few weeks disappeared and Helena knew she had been right to come so far to be with the man she loved.

There was no passionate embrace but his eyes said it all as he lifted her hand to his lips with old-world courtesy. Erica was wide-eyed as she regarded this tall handsome man in an elegant Chinese robe. Wasting no time Fu Yan bent to greet his little daughter stroking her face and producing a beautiful toy panda from behind his back. Erica was enchanted and happily took her father's hand as the little family moved down the train to collect the luggage.

Out of nowhere several rickshaw coolies appeared and the luggage was soon stowed securely and instructions given. Fu Yan then led them to a smarter vehicle of the same type and helped Helena and Erica into it. All three were smiling happily as the rickshaw set off, a perfect picture of family contentment. Fu Yan had Erica on his lap and held Helena's hand lovingly.

The roads became wider and calmer as the route led away from the stations and city centre and towards the university campus. Fu Yan had written that on his return from Germany he had been awarded a higher position in his Faculty and although Helena did not understand the academic set up she was happy and proud for him. As they passed the university he pointed out areas where he worked and taught and a few students they passed bowed respectfully to him.

In a few minutes more they turned into a narrower road and entered a large gateway with huge red doors. The luggage had already arrived and there was much clamour about unloading and seeking payment. Fu Yan took no part in all of this, simply helped Helena down and led them across the courtyard. Helena started to ask about the luggage but he brushed away the comments, saying that the servants would deal with it.

Glancing around the courtyard Helena saw that it was quite large with uneven brick underfoot and a number of dark doorways leading off. Fu Yan led them through one of these doorways into a dark cool passageway and across a brighter area into a large bedroom.

"This will be your room and Erica has a small room next door. Have a little rest and then I will come and introduce you to the family." With this he was gone and Helena stood quite nonplussed; she had expected that his family would be there to greet them and she had expected more show of affection from him. She supposed customs were different in China.

Towards the evening Fu Yan appeared at the door, took Erica's hand and led them out to a large room on the other side of the courtyard. The room was cool and dim; the shades pulled halfway down, and near to the fire on a low chair sat a small elderly lady. She had white hair severely drawn back from her face and wore a black silk Chinese robe embroidered in tan and fastened by ornate frog clasps. Her small bird-like eyes watched closely as the three approached and Helena knew herself to be under intense scrutiny. Fu Yan bowed slightly and spoke to his mother who held out a welcoming hand to Erica but only nodded to Helena. Although not understanding the ensuing conversation it was clear that Fu Yan's mother was as enchanted with Erica as he was. Helena began to feel a bit awkward but as usual revelled in the attention to Erica. Fu Yan translated the comments about how sweet and pretty the child was and then said, "Our honoured mother hopes that you and Erica will soon learn Mandarin." Helena smiled and nodded though she secretly feared that it would take her years to become confident in that language.

Fu Yan's mother waved a hand seemingly to dismiss them and reached down to pick up a small pipe lying on the table beside her. At that moment a younger woman stepped forward from the shadows across the room. She was perhaps in her forties very slim and traditionally dressed in a dark green robe. She did not smile but looked with interest at Helena and Erica. Fu Yan introduced her briefly to them giving her name as Mei Lee. He did not explain further so Helena guessed her to be his sister.

Back in their room, after putting Erica to bed next door, Helena and Fu Yan talked long into the night about all that had happened since they parted and about hopes and plans for the future. As far as day to day living was concerned Helena would have little to do but attend Mandarin classes because all cooking and cleaning was done by servants and Erica would have an Amah solely devoted to her. This was going to be such a change – a real culture shock!

At last Helena could not stifle a yawn; she was still really tired from the journey. Fu Yan rose and readily agreed that it was time for bed. He kissed her tenderly and then to her surprise said goodnight and walked to the door.

"Aren't you sleeping here?"

"No, I have my own room and anyway you are tired tonight. I will see you in the morning. Sleep well, my love."

Another strange custom, thought Helena. She had heard that even in Europe husband and wife might have separate rooms in large households but had not expected it here.

She undressed quickly and snuggled into the large bed which was very comfortable. After all that had happened she was tired enough to fall asleep in just a few minutes.

Next morning Helena woke to strange sounds of the household and lay for a few minutes reflecting on the difference in the layout of the house, so far removed from what she is used to. All the rooms gave off a central courtyard and corridor and there was no upstairs as far as she had seen. Next door all was quiet and she wondered that Erica, usually an early riser, had not already come to her Mama's bed.

Helena got out of bed and slipped into slippers to wake Erica for breakfast but the room was empty and panic clutched at heart. She ran back into her room to fetch a wrap just as Fu Yan came in carrying a large breakfast tray.

"Erica's gone!" she cried.

"Yes, it's alright, the Amah has taken her to have breakfast. Come, I've brought a German breakfast to make you feel at home."

Helena's heart stopped pounding but she didn't really feel happy that the child had been taken without her knowing.

Fu Yan set the breakfast down and they began to eat his version of German breakfast with the meats Helena had brought but with steamed white rolls and fragrant jasmine tea. As they ate Fu Yan explained his plans for the day which included a tour of the city's sights and the university. He explained he had taken a day to devote entirely to her and she expected how rare an occurrence this was to be.

After breakfast a rickshaw was called and Helena and Fu Yan set off on their sightseeing trip feeling like a honeymoon couple. Helena would have liked to take Erica along too but Fu Yan assured her that she was happily being cared for.

The day was mild and the sun shone so Helena wore a cream linen two-piece with the fashionable low waist line and pleated skirt. Fu Yan was in smart Western style clothes and many a head turned as they rode through the city. At first the roads were quite narrow in the mainly residential areas but soon they widened into some broader but still mainly unpaved thoroughfares. Everywhere was so busy and noisy and Helena realised now the reason for the thick walls and double nature of Fu Yan's home – now her home too. Fu Yan first took her to the Temple of Heaven where they left the rickshaw and strolled in the grounds. Helena thought she had never seen such a beautiful building with the elegant shaped roofs sparkling with gold and glinting in the sun.

Although nothing like a European church, the area still had a wonderfully serene atmosphere that made you want to whisper so as not to disturb the calm. Fu Yan bent and picked a small hibiscus flower and tucked it into Helena's hair. She felt herself melting with love for him and was so happy that their feelings for each other seemed just as strong as when they loved in Berlin.

Next on their list was the outer court of the Forbidden Palace with its pink walls and regal atmosphere. Fu Yan explained that only the outer part could be visited but when Helena asked whether the Emperor lived here all the time, he shushed her, saying it could be dangerous to talk about that. Near to the Forbidden Palace and Tiananmen Square was the famous Hotel de Pekin, where they stopped for some refreshments.

The hotel lounges were very elegant, furnished in a French style, and very busy with guests of all nationalities.

The last visit of the day was to the university where Fu Yan worked. It too consisted of many elegant buildings set in an extensive campus. As they strolled across the main courtyard several students bowed to Fu Yan and some older men greeted him but they did not seem to notice Helena.

As they drove back home Helena's mind and heart were full of all the fascinating sights and impressions of the day. She had lots to tell Erica over a meal of soup and vegetables.

Chapter 3

Over the next few weeks and months life settled into a pleasant routine for Helena and Erica. Each morning Helena attended the Mandarin class for foreigners, sometimes going by rickshaw but sometimes walking as it was not too far away in one of the university buildings.

Erica too was rapidly learning the language by talking with her Amah and playing with her young relatives who came to visit most days. The children enjoyed free rein of the house and courtyard apart from their grandma's apartment.

Every day or two Helena was expected to spend some time with Fu Yan's mother and Mei Lee who enjoyed playing with Erica. Sometimes however, the visits were hard to sustain as both women were in a dream-like state induced by the smoking of opium. Helena soon began to recognise the sweet smell of the smoke and tried to find reasons to postpone the visits. When not under the influence of the opiate Mei Lee was now very pleasant to Helena, often showing her the embroidery she was doing and helping to choose fabrics for new clothes because Fu Yan liked them all to dress in the Chinese fashion at home.

Fu Yan was only ever at home in the evening and there began to be some friction between them because he wanted Erica to stay up until he returned from the university and this was nearly always very late in the evening. He knew Erica's normal bed-time but, although he was clearly not teaching until so late, he regularly stayed talking with colleagues and visitors until way after dark. Helena asked him numerous times not to be too late but he took no notice, becoming irritated and insisting that these discussions were extremely important.

Helena didn't know what they could find to talk about for so many hours but realised that the political situation in China was causing anxiety in many quarters.

The Mandarin lessons were pretty much a saviour for Helena as they meant she was out each day with a definite purpose and she was meeting a lovely group of students, several of whom were young women in much the same position as herself. Without the classes Helena did not know what she would do all day as all the cooking and cleaning was done by servants and she was not really handy enough with a needle to sew or embroider. Once she wandered into the kitchen, thinking to help or maybe to learn some Chinese cooking – although she was struggling to get used to some of the odd and exotic flavours – but was more or less chased out by the cook who seemed to be offended that she was checking up on him.

There was little for her to do with regard to caring for Erica as she had the constant attention of her Amah whom she adored. Indeed the atmosphere and feeling in the house was still quite alien to Helena, for although no-one was unkind to her she felt they all still viewed her with suspicion.

The other ladies in the group also had plenty of spare time and they fell into the habit of visiting the Hotel de Pekin after lessons, where they could find a quiet corner in one of the elegant lounges and chat over tea or coffee when it was available. Although tempting to slip back into their own languages the girls were strict with themselves in trying to keep to Chinese whenever they could as they were all anxious to become fluent in their adopted tongue. The pleasure of the times they spent together soon developed into a firm friendship among the group.

On the few occasions when the others were busy Helena was invited to the home of Gerda, who was becoming a really special friend. Gerda was also married to a man who had studied in Germany and who now worked in the diplomatic service so their home was in the consular area of the city, not too far from Helena's. They chatted about how their lives had changed and sometimes wondered what the future would hold.

After one of these visits Helena decided to suggest to Fu Yan that they invite Gerda and her husband for an evening. He seemed quite amenable to the idea but did not suggest a date. The idea and the tentative plan cheered Helena but she still found it hurtful that Fu Yan often stayed so late at the university that she had gone to bed and he would spend the night in his own room. When he did return in the evenings, however, he was still very loving and attentive. Lately she was feeling tearful about their relationship and suspected she might be pregnant.

One of these lonely evenings Helena was woken by Erica standing in the doorway in tears. Expecting that she had a bad dream Helena cuddled her and began to take her back to bed but the child was shaking and running a high fever so she put her into the bigger bed and fetched some water from the jug to cool her. Helena sat in a chair beside the bed wiping Erica's hands and face with a damp flannel for about an hour but there was no improvement and the child seemed to be becoming delirious. Unsure what to do but very frightened Helena ran out of the room to fetch Fu Yan if he was home. His room was empty but his clothes lay discarded on a chair as if he had recently returned. Where could he be? She turned and was glad a moment later to see him coming out of the room opposite – Mei Lee's room. She quickly explained the situation and Fu Yan immediately took charge, despatching a servant to bring the doctor.

In no time at all a very old Chinese doctor appeared and briefly checked Erica's pulse and breathing. He grunted and spoke to Fu Yan handing him a strange looking piece of dried plant from his voluminous pockets. Apparently they had to make a tincture of this root and have Erica drink some every hour.

Erica's Amah was called to make the concoction and quickly returned with the murky looking medicine. Helena feared to give her this mixture but feared more not to. With some difficulty they persuaded Erica to take one or two sips of the stuff which she said was nasty. After that she slept for a time and the process was then repeated.

Helena and Fu Yan watched all night at Erica's bedside and were rewarded when, in the way of children, she was as bright in the morning as though nothing had happened. The happy parents embraced and Fu Yan went to get some breakfast for Erica while Helena closed her eyes and thought she had never seen a man more gentle and caring than her husband.

Although Erica seemed fully recovered Helena still wanted to keep a close eye on her and so missed her language classes for a few days.

The first day back to Mandarin classes Helena's friends greeted her, glad to see her back and talked about their relief that Erica had recovered so rapidly. Some had tales of similar situations and the odd medicines they or their children had endured, but with mainly good results.

After class Gerda asked Helena if she would go with her to a seamstress who was making her a new gown for a ball at the consulate and Helena readily agreed. As they strolled towards the tailors quarter of the city Helena told Gerda again of how concerned, kind and sympathetic Fu Yan had been during Erica's sickness, and she went on to talk about her proposed invitation to her and her husband for an evening dinner.

"It's rather difficult to arrange a time and date because my husband always works so late at the university, but I am sure we will be able to sort something out soon."

Gerda looked at Helena for a moment, bit her lip, and then said, "No, Helena dear, it won't happen."

Just then they arrived at the dressmaker's shop and Helena, though puzzled, knew she must wait to speak about it later.

The gown that was being prepared for Gerda was enchanting even though not completed. It was lilac silk, demurely cut and full length but the best part was the gorgeous orchids embroidered on the bodice. Helena thought it heavenly and felt quite envious. She decided then and there to mention this visit to Fu Yan and perhaps try to persuade him to buy her a gown by the same maker. On the way back to Gerda's house for some tea, Helena remembered Gerda's earlier comment and asked her what she had meant.

Gerda started to speak, then looked uncomfortable and hurried on saying, "We can't talk about it here."

At Gerda's house they sat on a wide cool veranda and waited while servants brought tea and marinated peanuts. Gerda poured the tea and taking a deep breath began, "You see in your situation it wouldn't be appropriate for you to be hostess."

"What do you mean, my situation?"

"You don't know, do you?"

"Know what?" Helena was completely perplexed.

"I'm sorry to be the one to explain, but I think it's only right. The woman you thought was Fu Yan's sister is his wife!"

There was a long silent moment while Gerda's words sank into Helena, turning her body cold and making her heart thud.

"That cannot be true, that cannot be true! How do you know?"

"My husband and Fu Yan studied together, they are old friends," replied Gerda. While Helena's teacup began to shake in her hand, Gerda continued to talk.

"Don't be too hard on him, it happens quite often here and you're certainly not alone. You know Helga in the group, she is in the same position."

"I don't believe you, Fu Yan would not lie to me like that!" Helena put down her teacup and almost ran out of the house. Gerda started to go after her feeling wretched that she had been the one to give her friend such a shock and afraid she had been too blunt, but how else did one say such things?

Helena hurried down the road, her heart was hammering in her chest and a burning pain was making it hard to breathe. It couldn't be true! It couldn't be true – could it?

Chapter 4

Back at the house Helena went straight to her room and closed the door, grateful for once that Erica was happily engaged with her Amah somewhere in the house. She stood stock still feeling numb from shock, horror and disbelief. After a time she sank onto the bed and put her head in her hands but no tears came, it was all too unreal too unbelievable for tears.

Fu Yan of course was not at home and would not be back for some hours but Helena's only rational thought was that she must see him and get the truth from him. She rose and walked around the room, hugging her arms around herself to contain her impatience and the turmoil of her feelings.

What would she do if it was true? No it couldn't be true, it just couldn't. After a time she felt she could wait no longer and determined to confront Fu Yan right away. Seeing nobody and in a blind nightmarish panic, she left the house and hurried towards the university campus. She did not know exactly where he would be but she had to find him before she went crazy.

Being late in the afternoon by this time the lecture rooms and offices were mostly quiet and as she walked across a peaceful quadrangle she realised she had no idea where to look. Part of her realised that she shouldn't have come and she was on the point of turning back to return home when she saw Fu Yan hurrying towards her looking very anxious.

"What are you doing here?" he asked. "Is there something wrong with Erica?"

"No, Erica's alright." Suddenly Helena couldn't speak for the pain in her chest and throat.

Fu Yan was angry that she had come to find him but as he waited for her to speak he could see the anguish in her face and some sixth sense told him – she knows! Without speaking he took her by the arm, none too gently, and they half walked, half ran back to the house.

Helena wanted to scream but by a supreme effort she waited until they were behind closed doors to shout the burning question. "Is Mei Lee your wife?" She expected denial. She hoped for reassurance but his response came as an anti-climax that astounded her.

"I thought you knew," said Fu Yan as he gently took her hand and led her to a chair. As soon as Helena recovered her faculties she snatched her hand away and at last her anger and fear poured out.

"How could I have known? How can you have two wives? You have lied to me, to my parents, to everyone!" She couldn't sit still a moment longer but jumped up and moved around room, wringing her hands.

"I never lied to you. In China the situation is different to Europe. My first marriage was a contract between our parents. When I met you I knew it was different."

Helena turned towards him, shaking her head and uttering, "No, no I can't believe you've treated me like this. How could you?" At last the tears that were pent up over the last few hours could wait no longer and Helena broke down, sobbing helplessly. Fu Yan made to comfort her but she shook him off and still weeping violently, she pushed him towards the door shouting "Go, go away, go to her!"

As the heavy door banged behind him, Helena sank onto her bed totally exhausted by the turmoil of her emotions and pent up fury. She lay for some time unable to believe how her life had come to this and unable to stop shaking. After a time she fell asleep and dreamed a sweet dream of Fu Yan bringing her Lily of the Valley in Berlin, but she woke in the early hours of the morning stiff with cold to remember the reality she now had to deal with.

At first light Helena dragged two suitcases out of the closet, one large and one smaller, and started to think about what to pack. She would only be able to take essentials and anyway she'd only take European things, she wanted no more reminder of China. In a little while Erica came in with a tousled head and a sweet smile. After a hug she looked at the cases and said, "Are we going somewhere Mama?"

"We're going back to Germany darling."

Erica thought for a moment and then started pouting "I don't want to go to Germany, I like it here. I've got new clothes, my Amah, and Papa calls me his princess."

Helena had been concerned that Erica was becoming spoilt with all the attention she received in a house full of servants, and here was the proof.

Wishing to avoid a tantrum and too weary to cajole she settled for the parental standby: "We'll see". The Amah then came to collect Erica for her breakfast and took her away without making any comment about the packing. As soon as they left Helena again sagged into a chair and began to realise that she had little money of her own and no way of buying a ticket to travel. She couldn't ask Fu Yan for money although he had always been very generous to her. The only thing to do was to ask Gerda for help, maybe she or her husband could arrange passage for them.

She left the packing and started to get ready for the language class, putting on her best dress and spending some time trying to repair the effects of crying and little sleep on her face. Helena never wore much make-up but a cold flannel and some face powder helped. She left for class without breakfast and without seeing anyone in the house.

Although she found it hard to concentrate, the lesson did take her mind off things for a while. After class Gerda, who had been watching her during the session, immediately took he arm and led her to a quiet garden in part of the campus.

"Are you alright Helena? I'm so sorry I had to tell you but I thought you needed to know."

Helena ignored that and came straight to the point, "I'm leaving him, can you help me to get a ticket, Gerda?"

Gerda was shocked at the coldness of her friend's voice but understood the sentiment. "Don't do that Helena, he loves you and you love him. You just have to adjust to the situation. Why don't you talk to Helga. Find out how she coped. I'm sure you can work it out."

"No, I don't want to talk to Helga or anyone. I can never forgive him. I'm leaving. If you won't help me I'll find someone who can." Helena started to walk away but Gerda followed and hugged her saying, "I'll help you with whatever I can, I promise."

Helena smiled weakly and started to walk home. She soon found herself in streets she didn't recognise and realised that in her stress she had walked and walked without knowing where she was going. A European woman was very conspicuous in this area and she began to feel very uncomfortable. Steeling herself not to run and become more conspicuous she rounded a corner and with relief recognised the back of the Hotel de Pekin which meant she could get her bearings.

At last back at the house, Helena began to feel faint and realised she had not eaten for twenty four hours so she called a servant and asked for some soup. Even in her current state of mind she knew she must keep strong for herself and her child no, children; for she was sure now that she carried a second.

Helena spent the afternoon in her room alternating between despair and anger, sometimes sitting with her head in her hands, sometimes pacing the room. Eventually she started again to pack the suitcases and gather her few valuable possessions. It occurred to her that she could perhaps sell some belongings to get money for a ticket if all else failed. The day wore on and of course there was no sign of Fu Yan. Her life was in pieces and he'd just gone to the university.

Sometime later came a knock at the door and Helena opened it to see Fu Yan bearing a tray of food. "My mother says you've hardly eaten all day."

"I don't want anything." Helena turned away and thought again how amazing it was that the old woman rarely stirred from her rooms but always knew exactly what went on in the house.

"May I come in?" asked Fu Yan.

Helena just shrugged and sat down feeling bone weary, hopeless and drained. Fu Yan immediately noticed the bags and roughly asked, "What are you doing."

"You can see what I'm doing. I'm packing. I'm going back to Germany."

"You can't do that! You and Erica belong here – we are a family!"

"No, Fu Yan I can't live this way. It's wrong and you deceived me."

"It's the Chinese way. I would have told you but I didn't think you would understand. You've been happy here, haven't you?"

"I won't stay with you, you are a bigamist."

"Helena, please, what can I do to make you change your mind?"

"Nothing, Helena replied "I've made up my mind and you can't stop me!"

"Oh, yes I can." Fu Yan muttered ominously, and with that he snatched up Helena's passport from the bedside table and threw it in the fire.

"What are you doing?" cried Helena as she rushed to retrieve it from the flames. But Fu Yan caught her arm and pulled her away. They struggled but he was too strong and soon the precious document was ashes.

Helena broke away, shaking with fury. She could hardly believe he'd done that. Captain Petrovsky's revolver was in the suitcase. She took it out and turned to Fu Yan. "I'll kill you! – I'll kill you!" she cried, and pointed the gun straight at his heart. Fu blanched visibly but did not move.

For long moments they stared at each other while Helena struggled with such mixed emotions as she could never have believed. The gun was heavy and her hand began to shake. Fu Yan seized the opportunity to grab the gun and wrestle it from her grasp.

Drained and weeping uncontrollably Helena sank onto the bed while Fu Yan put the revolver on the far side of the room. He came over and reached to touch her but Helena shook him off.

In those few moments while she held the gun on him she had realised she still loved him, but that didn't mean she could forgive him.

Chapter 5

The realisation that she was completely trapped sent Helena into deep despair. For the next day or two she hardly left her room, hardly ate, didn't even dress properly. No-one in the household came to see her except sweet little Erica who brought toys and games to try to cheer her Mama. Fu Yan came once in the evening bringing some chrysanthemum tea, presumably as a peace offering. They were civil to each other but no more and there was no mention of the gun, which he had taken away, or the passport.

Next day the Amah gently knocked her door and told Helena she had a visitor. She was followed in by Gerda carrying a beautiful box of orchids. The sight of her friend bearing such a gift was almost too much for Helena and she had to fight away the tears as Gerda hugged her and stroked her back.

After a few minutes Gerda went into organising mode, sorting out a lovely outfit for Helena to wear with matching accessories and helping her to arrange her hair in a pretty modern way. She chattered all the time explaining that they were meeting `the girls` for tea at the fabulous new

Tea House on the Shichahai Lakes near the Forbidden City.

"Helga will be there," said Gerda, "but if you don't want to say anything you don't have to."

Helena took a deep breath and started to tell her friend about the confrontation she had had with Fu Yan but the words would not come and Gerda stopped her saying, "Don't distress yourself, we'll talk about it later."

So, dressed to kill, the ladies headed off to hire a rickshaw to take them to the appointed meeting with their precious ex-pat friends.

In the rickshaw Gerda whispered, "I hope you don't mind but I did tell Helga about your problem. But you needn't worry she's very discreet."

Helena opened her mouth to say, "You had no right," but realised that her friend only meant to be supportive so she just nodded.

At the Tea House Helena and Gerda were greeted by the small group of friends assembled and several remarked on how charming Helena looked today. Tea and pastries were ordered and all were delighted to find that the chef had the knowledge and skill to prepare light European style pastries that were rarely available in Peking. The food was delicious and the conversation wide ranging but light and happy so that the time passed quickly and pleasantly.

Gradually the party broke up as some ladies had other appointments to go to and Helena found herself next to Helga who suggested a stroll around the lake with a meaningful glance at her friend. Helena agreed and they set off arm in arm.

"If you don't want to talk I'll understand," said Helga, after a while, "but I may be able to help you, Helena."

Helena said nothing for a while then thought to begin by asking Helga about her own situation, "How did you find out about your husband's first marriage?"

"He told me straight away, as soon as I arrived in China. It was a real shock, I can tell you. Well, you know how it knocks you for six. His first wife and her children were in one part of the house and I was in another to begin with."

"Why didn't you leave him?" asked Helena.

"I had nowhere to go." replied Helga. "My father was killed in the war and my mother remarried a man who thought he'd got two for the price of one. Any time he could he tried to get at me. I narrowly escaped being raped by him more than once, so whatever happened here was better than going back to that."

"That's awful," said Helena. As they walked on for a bit before she began to explain a bit about her situation. Helga listened, putting questions in now and then. Finally Helena started to cry again, saying "I just don't think I can forgive him for deceiving me but I don't know what to do."

They stopped and sat on a wooden bench while Helena dried her eyes on an embroidered handkerchief. When she had calmed herself Helga sought to clarify the situation by asking, "So Fu Yan's wife is older than you and she has no children?"

"That's right, I think so anyway," replied Helena.

"Well, that's it then, he married you to have children because a Chinese man must have children to prove his manhood. You can have children and obviously she can't so you have a clear advantage. If I were you I would use that advantage to enjoy life here as much as possible."

The two women chatted a bit longer about the life and culture that they have come to and when they parted Helena felt a lot more positive.

On the way home she made a metal list of conditions that she would put to Fu Yan. Helga had advised her to keep quiet about her pregnancy for the time being and allayed her fears that she would not love the child because it had been conceived in deception.

Next morning to Helena's surprise, Fu Yan appeared at the door smartly dressed in European style and announced that he had taken some leave and would like to invite her on a little trip to the Great Wall. Helena was secretly pleased but she accepted coolly and said she would be ready in an hour or so.

As they travelled out of the city Fu Yan fussed over her as though he were wooing her again but Helena remained aloof. He wasn't going to get off that easily. The scenery was breath taking and Helena really did enjoy the cleaner air away from the city. After admiring the spectacular views and strolling (two feet apart) along the wall, they went on to a small village where Fu Yan had some contacts. In a delightful secluded courtyard he had arranged for a superb meal to be served to them. There were foreign delicacies and delicious wine.

After the meal and a couple of glasses of wine, Helena decided to put her ultimatum forward.

"I will stay and be your wife but I want to have more input into how the household is run and I want a proper European style marriage. That means we have a room together and you make opportunities for us to entertain friends and colleagues. Do you agree?"

To Helena's amazement Fu Yan meekly agreed to all her conditions and reach across the table to hold her hand before lifting it to his lips and taking from his pocket a small silken box. This he held out to her asking forgiveness and declaring his love in a most ardent way.

The box contained a beautiful golden brooch in the form of a Sakura tree with rubies representing the blossom and delicate enamelled love-birds on a branch. Fu Yan explained that the Sakura tree is a Chinese love symbol and he carefully pinned it to Helena's lapel. The whole ambience was totally romantic but Helena was determined not to let herself be won over too easily. She smiled and thanked him for she was genuinely delighted with such a gorgeous piece of jewellery. On the way home he offered his arm and she took it but still in quite a formal way.

On their arrival back at home Erica ran to meet them with lots of happy chatter and news. Fu Yan's delight and pride in his little daughter was very evident and it was good to see the two of them playing together. Helena's heart began to soften a little and she reflected that in spite of the awful shock she had sustained, this life she had chosen was potentially full and rewarding if not entirely what she had expected. She remembered the doubts and fears she had suffered during the long journey to China and felt a tentative pride that she had overcome those and this latest set-back. She would still keep the news of her pregnancy quiet for a bit longer as fortunately she felt quite well and was not yet showing. As Helga had explained she held a trump card and she mustn't waste it. She couldn't help wondering though how she would feel about intimate relations with her husband after all this.

The promises Fu Yan had made about household changes were honoured: soon the rooms were re-arranged so that they shared a bedroom and he had clearly spoken to the cook for the next time Helena ventured into the kitchen she had a very different reception. She was able to watch and learn some of the cooking techniques and to introduce some German dishes. Although she was aware that the cook tried to shield them from the view of the 'Kitchen God' plaque.

As her pregnancy advanced, Helena began to think about the birth, imagining she would have a home delivery which didn't bother her. But the memory of the ancient Chinese doctor who had visited Erica and the vile tincture he had prescribed gave her cause for concern. These worries were shared one morning with her friends from the language group and one of them immediately came up with a wonderful solution, for she knew of an American couple, a doctor and his wife, who had recently set up a small practice in an area not far from the university. This lady assured Helena that the doctor was really well qualified and knew the most modern techniques. Helena took note of the man's name and address and decided to speak to Fu Yan quite soon; she knew that when she told him about the baby he would agree to anything she wanted.

Next day after a late supper, at which Helena had eaten very little rice and some egg due to the fact that in her current condition late meals gave her heartburn at night, she revealed her news. Fu Yan was overjoyed as she had expected and was quite surprised when she told him how advanced the pregnancy was. When he asked why she hadn't told him before she simply said she wanted to be sure in case anything went wrong.

Helena immediately brought up the question of the American doctor, saying that he had been recommended to her by a friend, and Fu Yan readily agreed to book an appointment to meet him and hopefully engage his services.

Dr Gene Chapman was duly contacted and invited with his wife to the house to meet Fu Yan and Helena. He was very pleased to have been contacted by a leading member of the university, not really realising that it was on a professional matter. A time was made for the appointment and Helena reminded Fu Yan several times when the doctor and his wife were due so that he would not forget and remain at college as he still often did.

Tea and fruit was prepared for the visit and Helena felt delight in presiding as hostess for the little gathering. Small talk was somewhat limited due to language problems but still the company was pleasant. Erica peeped in at one point and provided the perfect opportunity for the subject of Helena's pregnancy to be brought up. The doctor was flattered that he had been recommended by Helena's friends and an appointment at his practice was made for a preliminary examination. Gene's wife Chrissie was a warm and friendly girl who quickly developed a rapport with Helena, who invited her to the language group's next outing.

The doctor's appointment a few days later went well; he worked out an approximate date for the birth and agreed to be on hand for the delivery.

The question of a suitable midwife was discussed as he said Chrissie could help or he knew of an older Chinese lady who was very experienced. Helena thought the best solution was to leave the choice to him. When she returned and told Fu Yan about it all he said, "Oh no, the Amah will attend you as always, that goes without saying!"

Chapter 6

A day or two later Helena was summoned to her mother-in-law's room; feeling like a naughty school girl, she made her way through the house, wondering as she went whether the old lady was still her mother-in-law.

Fu Yan's mother was seated bolt upright in her chair and made no move to greet Helena as she entered. Without pre-amble and with lips as tight as leather she said "Fu Yan tells me you are pregnant! Why did you not tell me first? That is what you should always do". Helena's grasp of the language had improved so well that she could understand clearly the outburst but even if she had not been able to, the woman's demeanour would have conveyed the message that she was seriously displeased.

Helena did not see why she should apologise so she simply said, "I thought you would be pleased".

The older woman ignored this and went on with her second complaint, "I understand you have also seen a foreign doctor. You have much to learn about our ways. You will be attended by the Amah and our doctor if necessary. We do not want a foreign medicine man in this house!" She looked away and dismissed Helena with a wave of her hand.

This infuriated Helena and she almost burst into tears on the spot but managed to suppress it until she reached her room. After weeping and shaking for some minutes Helena calmed herself for the sake of the unborn child and considered this new turn of events. It was clear that the new-found power she thought she had over Fu Yan by virtue of the pregnancy was actually non-existent.

Later in the day Helena was meeting up with 'the girls' for tea and conversation, which happily took her mind off her problems for a while.

At one point during the afternoon one of the ladies, a lively extravagant woman called Irmgard was complaining in a frivolous way that the allowance she had from her husband simply did not cover all the new dresses she needed. The group laughed with her knowing that she would find a way to access the poor man's wallet but in Helena's mind an idea started to form as she pondered a way to secure some independence for herself and her children.

Gerda had noticed that Helena seemed quieter than usual so, as they left the tea garden, she linked arms with Helena and asked, "Are you ok? You were very quiet this afternoon." Helena told her about the interview with her mother-in-law and confessed that she was really unhappy that she would not be allowed to be attended by Dr Chapman.

"Look," said Gerda, after thinking for a while, "It's your second baby so long as everything goes well you shouldn't have much need for a doctor. Let's go and see Gene and ask what he thinks."

They arranged to go together to the doctor's house directly after the next language lesson. Helena was glad Gerda would be there to help explain as her knowledge of English was quite good.

Leaving the classroom with Gerda three days later Helena felt furtive and almost guilty but Gerda brusquely reminded her that she had to think about her health and her baby.

At the doctors house they were shown into a neat waiting room for just a short time until Gene became available.

Helena's anxiety and distress were obvious to the doctor but he didn't ask the reason until he had briefly checked her pulse and temperature in his calm and professional way. When Helena began to explain her situation, with some help from Gerda, Dr Chapman sat back in his chair and steeled his fingers. He was not really surprised but he was disappointed as he had been delighted to be consulted by an important member of the university. Ever since setting up his practice in China he had been encountering this prejudice and suspicion of foreigners that is endemic in the Chinese culture.

It had not been overt, of course; Chinese people were unfailingly courteous and polite, but at heart, for most of them, the old ways persisted.

Helena was so afraid that he would be insulted but he was not and he reassured her that he would still be happy to keep a check on her during her pregnancy and be available for the birth in the event of any complications.

"There you are," said Gerda, "you can come for your check-ups after lessons or you can say that you are coming to visit me."

This solution seemed the best available and Helena returned home feeling much better.

Now for the next part of her plan!

She first headed to the kitchen to arrange with the cook for some of Fu Yan's favourite dishes to be prepared. Next she washed and dried her hair, put on one of his favourite dresses, pinned on the ruby brooch and sat down to wait for her husband's return. He was later than expected but Helena had become used to this by now.

On greeting Helena, Fu Yan was delighted to see how pretty she looked and pleased to sit down to a really tasty meal. During supper the couple chatted amicably and Fu Yan was secretly feeling very pleased that Helena seemed to have got over the shock of his first wife and to have accepted the situation.

She had not!

After supper Helena began to talk about the new baby, reminding him that that she would need to buy a number of special items in preparation. He of course agreed and asked how much she would need. This was her opportunity to suggest it would be more sensible if she had a personal allowance rather than just ad hoc amounts. At first Fu Yan seemed unsure but Helena continued explaining that she needed some maternity dresses and would like to invite her friends from time to time. He considered for a few moments and then agreed, mentioning a sum that was far more than Helena had anticipated. She was delighted but did not show it, just accepted gracefully. With that amount she would be able to save quite quickly and plan for her escape sometime in the future. She must find a safe place to keep spare cash and she knew that with the political and economic situation as it was in China, currency could possibly de-value overnight so it would be necessary to purchase gold as a safety net.

Helena's pregnancy proceeded naturally and problem free. She visited Dr Chapman every few weeks for a check-up when he checked her blood pressure, her weight and the foetal heartbeat. Although still rather unhappy about the deception involved in visiting the American doctor, Helena felt very well and confident that Gene had promised he would be on hand in needed.

Dr Chapman had worked out an approximate date for the birth and with uncharacteristic punctuality, on that very date Helena woke in the night with backache and a feeling of nausea. She waited a while to see if it improved but quite quickly the backache became definite contractions. Fu Yan was roused and immediately went into expectant father mode, pacing around while Helena and the Amah calmly prepared the room for the birth.

Dawn came, then midday, then the next evening and still Helena's contractions were severe but no baby had appeared. Around seven in the evening Helena glanced at the Amah and saw panic in her eyes. She knew then that help was needed and she screamed at Fu Yan to fetch Dr Chapman. Although he knew he should obey his mother and send for a Chinese doctor, Fu Yan respected Helena's wishes and sent a servant running to Dr Chapman.

Thankfully the doctor arrived very quickly and immediately sought to calm Helena while he assessed the situation. He had experienced such a case while in America when newly trained and hoped he would be able to resolve the problem. The best thing would be to give Helena a tiny whiff of chloroform to relieve the pain briefly and enable him to ease the baby back into the birth canal slightly and loosen the cord that seem to be in the way.

The chloroform smelt sickly-sweet but in a moment Helena was woozy and before she knew it Dr Chapman was urging her to push and the baby was born at last. It was a baby boy with a shock of black hair and basically healthy but in some distress due to the prolonged labour.

The Amah took the child from the doctor and calmly and efficiently washed and wrapped him before handling him to Helena. With the euphoria of relief she gazed at her little son's serious face, holding him close until very soon they both slept.

Chapter 7

Helena woke to hear excited whispering and, as she opened her eyes, Fu Yan, clutching a huge bouquet in one hand and little Erica with the other, crept carefully towards the bed. Though still tired she smiled happily as she saw both father and the baby's sister peer excitedly into the bamboo crib, where the tightly-wrapped baby slept.

After a few moments Fu Yan turned to her with a loving smile and tears in his eyes.

"He is so beautiful. You've made me so proud," he whispered and bent to kiss Helena's forehead, then her hand.

Erica realised they were whispering because the baby slept but in her excitement hers was more of a stage whisper, "When can I hold him?" she ask. The parents shushed her but she had inadvertently bumped a bit against the cot and the child began to stir.

After helping Helena to sit up in bed Fu Yan said he would call the Amah to help with the baby but Helena said, "No, you can pick him up." She was determined that this time he would be fully involved with the baby-care which he had avoided last time by returning to China. Taking a deep breath, Fu Yan nervously gathered the whimpering bundle into his arms and she could see he was visibly moved. Erica clamoured to be allowed to hold him but he said only if she sat down, so she immediately plonked herself down on the floor.

Helena laughed, "No darling, come and sit here." Patting the bed beside her, Erica climbed onto the bed and sat beside her Mama, and held out her arms. Fu Yan carefully placed the baby on his sister's lap and leant to embrace all three of them.

"What's his name?" asked Erica, as she rocked him a little, actually hoping to wake him up.

Fu Yan looked at Helena enquiringly as she answered, "I thought Manfred would suit him very well. What do you think?"

"Whatever you think my dear, Manfred will be perfect."

As though on cue at hearing his name, the little boy screwed his face and let out a lusty cry. Erica began to rock him harder but he didn't stop and she was relieved that Helena took him from her. Having heard the baby cry the Amah came in and hustled the visitors out of the room so that Helena could feed the child.

Trying to feed the screaming infant was a struggle and both mother and child became distressed but Helena tried to keep calm remembering that with Erica it had taken several days for feeding to become comfortably established. Eventually Manfred must have achieved some nourishment or wore himself out so that he slept. The Amah cleaned and settled him in the crib and as she left the room to attend to her other duties Helena heard her say, "Never mind we will soon have some help for you both."

"What do you mean?" called Helena.

"Well I am sure your mother will arrange for a wet nurse," she replied. "It is the custom in good families," she added when she saw

Helena's shocked expression.

Now Helena was in turmoil. She had been so delighted that Fu Yan had immediately accepted her choice of name for the child, a German name meaning strength and peace, but now it seemed there would be further confrontation with her mother-in-law as there was no way she would accept another woman feeding her child.

She picked up the lovely bouquet that Fu Yan had laid on the bed earlier and went to put it aside when she noticed a small silk purse hidden among the flowers. Opening it revealed a stunning emerald and diamond ring that must have cost a fortune. Helena could not resist trying it on and it fitted.

As she lay back to rest again she couldn't help wondering if Fu Yan would support her against his mother this time or if the old matriarch was too powerful.

All too soon the baby woke again and began to demand food. Helena was happy to see Fu Yan entering the room rather than the servant and he was carrying a smart new cradle.

"I didn't like to see our beautiful son in that cheap bamboo cot so I got this much nicer one for him."

It was indeed fit for a prince, lacquered and decorated in traditional style. Helena loved it but suspected that if the child had been a girl, the bamboo would have sufficed. She made no comment on that, however, and just smiled as Fu Yan took her hand.

"I see you found the birthday ring, my darling."

"Yes, it's gorgeous, thank you."

They kissed and Fu Yan went on to explain that the ring will become a family heirloom as Helena keeps it only until Manfred's wife has her first son, when it passes on to her.

"Oh," Helena was a little disappointed. "There seem to be so many customs I must get used to."

Tears welled in her eyes as she started to tell her husband about the wet nurse situation.

"I will never allow another woman to feed him, even if it is difficult at the moment."

Fu Yan could see how distressed she was and sought to calm her saying "It's alright, you must do what you think is right. I'm sure my mother will understand; I'll fetch her to meet her grandson."

As he left, Helena sighed deeply and tried to dry her eyes. She picked up and rocked the baby while she waited in trepidation.

At length the old lady and Mei Lee appeared and, to Helena's horror, Fu Yan just left them at the door and disappeared. Both women, however, cooed and fussed over the little boy and were very complimentary about his beauty and his strength. Mei Lee asked to hold him and seemed unable to take her eyes off him.

In due course, while the three women drank some special herb tea, Helena's mother-in-law raised the issue of the wet nurse, saying how it would help Helena to regain her strength. Her final comment was, "I'm sure Fu Yan was wrong in saying you didn't want it."

"No, Mother-in-law, he was right. I will not have anyone else feed my baby."

The old woman's mouth tightened into a thin line and her eyes took on a harsh glitter.

"You seem to be determined to hold on to all your foreign ways," she spat out and hobbled out of the room gesturing for Mei Lee to go with her.

Helena sank back onto the pillows and began to cry again; since the birth, the slightest thing seemed to make her tearful. In a few minutes, Erica came in with a story book and Helena rallied, cheering up a bit as they read the story together.

Over the next few days a sort of routine was established with the baby but Helena still felt miserable and weary all the time. Fu Yan wasn't at home much because he had told her he was involved in many important meetings at the university, regarding the possibility of moving to a safer region if the political revolution became too dangerous.

Surprisingly, Helena's most welcome companion over these days was the gentle Mei Lee who clearly adored the child and tried to comfort Helena when she became upset.

Helena felt she had a dark chasm inside her and however much she tried to feel happy and positive, it would not go away. Outside of the family she had no visitors and she hardly ate anything but plain rice and some awful tea that was supposed to help her milk production.

One day, a week or so later, while Mei Lee was softly crooning to the child, Helena confided to her that she was so upset that none of her friends had come to see her and the baby. Mei Lee looked uncomfortable and quickly changed the subject, bringing the baby over for a feed.

The very next day there was some commotion in the hallway outside Helena's room and when she opened the door it was Gerda!

"Oh I'm so happy to see you, please come in," called Helena.

Gerda was laden with gifts and flowers for mother and baby from herself and Helena's other friends in their circle. The first thing she said was, "I'm so sorry, I wanted to come last week but they wouldn't let me in. Dr Chapman tried to visit as well and he was refused entry. Are you O.K? You look a bit peaky."

"Who wouldn't let you come?"

"The doorman and the other servants must have had instructions to allow no visitors. We were all very worried about you."

The two women embraced and Helena burst into tears. Through her sobs Helena whispered, "That woman is so evil, she is trying to keep us away from all foreign influences and I've been feeling so down, I wished and wished you'd come."

In Gerda's comforting hands, Helena recovered after a while and she explained to her all the trouble about the wet nurse adding, "I feel so weak and depressed, I'm just a mess."

"I'll bring the doctor tomorrow even if we have to knock the door down!"

Gerda's visit cheered Helena no end. They spent most of the afternoon exclaiming over the gifts and, of course, adoring the baby. As she left Gerda promised faithfully to return the next day and Helena felt more cheerful than she had been for ages.

Next day Dr Chapman examined Helena, talked to her about a condition called post-natal depression, or "baby blues," and prescribed some tonic which he said would help.

Gradually over the next few weeks Helena's health and mood returned to normal with the help of her friends and the good doctor. She was able to resume some of her language lessons and make the occasional visit to a friend or one of their favourite tea gardens. As Helena was still feeding the baby she made sure to be away for only a short time and was confident that the Amah and Mei Lee kept a careful eye on him. Mei Lee frequently spent peaceful hours just watching him in his cradle.

Erica, too, became rather more demanding, obviously feeling some jealousy over all the attention her baby brother was getting, so Helena gave as much time and effort as she could to redress the balance. One of their favourite outings was to a nearby market where Erica enjoyed watching the live birds and animals, not realising that they were destined for the cooking pot. The visit always finished with a treat to eat on the way home, usually a sort of fruit kebab, rather like a toffee-apple but consisting of a variety of exotic fruits.

Returning from one of these trips Helena removed her hat and washed her hands, sticky from the fruit, before peeping in to see if Manfred had yet woken from his afternoon nap. She was surprised that he wasn't there and neither of his "guardians," were around. It was usually easy to locate the Amah but she was not in her usual places. At last Helena did find her in Erica's room sitting with her head in her hands, rocking and wailing.

Immediately she knew something was wrong!

"Where's my baby?" she screamed.

The woman was shaking as she replied "I tried to stop her but I couldn't. Mei Lee has taken him."

Panic gripped Helena as she tried to make sense of this and find out where she had gone. Without any clear idea of where to look, Helena ran out of the house and to the corner of the road. By some miracle Fu Yan was walking down the road towards home, very unusual at this time of the day. Catching sight of his distraught wife he ran to her and she quickly explained that the baby had gone

"Where can he be?" Helena sobbed, holding tightly to him.

Fu Yan thought for a moment, then said, "Let's try the lake." Together they ran across the university campus, surprising a few students who were just leaving classes.

The lake was not large but well hidden among bamboo and bushes. Fu Yan started to call out and as they reached the clearing above the lake they both stood stock still.

Mei Lee was wading into the lake holding the child but as she heard her name called she turned and seemed to lose her footing. Still holding the baby tightly she struggled to regain her balance but in a moment Fu Yan had thrown himself into the water, grabbed for his son and soon held him firmly, leaving Mei Lee to fight for her own survival in the muddy waters.

Grim-faced he returned near enough to shore to pass Helena the baby, saying, "Take him home."

Helena had no intention of doing otherwise and she hurried away without a backward glance. Once home the Amah helped her to dry and change the screaming, soaked little mite, with tears of relief pouring down both their faces. He had come to no harm and was soon pacified with a feed. Vowing to herself never to leave him again, Helena laid him down to sleep and found herself nodding off too in the chair after all the emotional turmoil.

She was woken by Fu Yan gently touching her arm. His clothes were still sopping wet and streaked with mud but they clung together for several minutes while Helena assured him that the baby was fine.

Normally most fastidious in dress, Fu Yan ignored the mess he was in and sank down on the bed while he relayed what had happened at the lake.

He told her that he went back into the lake and managed after a struggle to get Mei Lee back to shore but she didn't seem to think she had done anything wrong.

Helena didn't speak but began to shake again at the thought of what could have happened.

"It seems her mind has gone," said Fu Yan "It will not happen again as I have told her she must return to her parent's home. She will not be allowed back until she is well again."

Chapter 8

Next day Gerda arrived for tea, as arranged, bringing with her some delicious little pastries; they were rather like baklava but made with red bean paste and sesame seeds.

Helena was unsure whether she ought to tell her friend about the awful upset of the previous day since Fu Yan might consider it a private family matter but Gerda already knew something had happened and was bursting to know the ins and outs.

After tasting the tea and pastries Gerda sat back and with some exasperation said, "Well come on tell me what happened." There was no doubt as to what she was referring to, especially when she explained that Fu Yan and his wife had been seen coming back to the house in a wet and bedraggled state.

Actually it was a relief to Helena to pour out the stressful details of yesterday's incident, reliving as she did so the panic she had felt then and in the middle of the night, when she woke several times with her heart pounding. Gerda, a mother herself, readily empathised and moved forward to hold and soothe her friend.

"He's alright though, isn't he?" she asked, to soothe Helena and reassure herself.

"Yes, he's fine, but I just can't help imagining what might have happened."

"I know, it's just awful. Where is Mei Lee now?"

"Oh, Fu Yan said she couldn't stay here in case it happened again. He sent her back to her parents. I just can't understand why she did that, she seemed to love Manfred so much."

"Mmm, I wouldn't be surprised if the opium was actually to blame," suggested Gerda. "I have heard that its use can really affect a person's thinking and sanity."

Although that wasn't a pleasant thought to Helena, it did explain some things and helped to make sense of the situation.

After a few more tears, the friends took some more tea and, by unspoken consent, tried to talk of other things. Inevitably these included their children. Gerda had two boys and one girl a little older than Erica but while the boys were attending a good school and doing well, the little girl remained at home. Helena had recently gone with Fu Yan to make enquiries at the convent school near the university, wondering how soon the nuns would be able to take Erica as a day pupil only. This came up in the conversation and Gerda sighed, bit her lip and said "You see you're really lucky in that way. My husband is more of the old Chinese School which regards it a waste to educate girls above the most elementary level."

"But that's outrageous in this day and age!"

"I know, but I've tried to argue against the tradition and got nowhere, I'm surprised your mother-in-law is allowing it."

"Mmm," mused Helena, "I wonder if she knows. I hope we're not in for another confrontation."

Gerda gathered her things together to leave after a little cuddle and pet with the baby. As they said goodbye, Helena hesitantly asked for assurance that the incident with Mei Lee and their suspicions would go no further.

"Of course not, my dear, I promise I wouldn't say anything!"

It soon became clear that Fu Yan's colleagues at the university knew about the situation with Mei Lee and possibly about the incident, although Helena was sure Fu Yan wouldn't have said much; he was a very private person in many ways and regarded family matters as essentially private.

Helena and Fu Yan began to get invitations from the other lecturers and professors; at first for tea or cocktails and later to dinners and even a banquet. Helena was so pleased that she had worked hard at the Mandarin lessons and continued to practice whenever she could, for she found that she was able to converse quite well with their hosts and their wives. This made Fu Yan very proud of her and he mentioned several times how impressed his colleagues were with her command of the Chinese language.

When the invitation to the banquet arrived Fu Yan asked Helena if she would like a new dress for the occasion and, never one to refuse a gift horse, she readily agreed.

"Perhaps my mother could go with you to the dressmaker? I know she'd really like to, she is sorely missing the company of Mei Lee."

Helena would much rather have gone with Gerda but she didn't see how she could refuse so, next day, after waiting an age for the old woman to get ready, they set off in a rickshaw. Although Helena didn't have her friend with her, she knew exactly where she wanted to go: to the dressmaker who had sewn that gorgeous lilac dress for Gerda, so she called out the address to the coolie. Mother-in-law looked very surprised and said, "I thought we were going to my dressmaker."

"Well, we can go there afterwards if you like."

Disapproval was thick in the air but Helena made her mind up to pretend she hadn't noticed. At the dressmaker's shop she helped the old lady down and settled her in a chair beside the counter with the help of a young shop assistant. The dressmaker herself, quickly appeared and made much of her elderly customer, bringing her tea and a plate of fruit. The grim line of her mother-in-law's mouth softened a little at all the fuss being made of her.

The tailoress recognised Helena as Gerda's friend and was well aware that she must be the wife or concubine of someone well-to-do. Guessing correctly that Helena was after something similar to the dress she had made for Gerda, the small Chinese woman asked if the dress was for a special occasion. Helena explained about the banquet and was not reticent about 'name-dropping' the elegant venue and the host's name.

Duly impressed, the seamstress thought for a moment and then produced several bolts of glorious silk fabric from a nearby cupboard. Helena and mother-in-law stroked the fabrics appreciatively while the dressmaker's assistant held each one against Helena's skin to help choose the colour. At length they had chosen two shades: a warm peachy apricot and a stunning sapphire blue, but it felt impossible to choose between them so throwing caution to the wind, she cried "I'll take both!"

The older lady looked very surprised but said nothing and Helena realised that it was not that she thought she should have two dresses, rather that to insist upon only one would look as though the family could only afford one. The fierce pride of the Chinese character could sometimes work to one's advantage!

The dressmaker rapidly made notes of Helena's measurements and an appointment was made for a fitting. Then the rickshaw was called back and they went onto the second establishment. Here it was clear that the prevalent styles were much more traditional though the fabrics were rich and generally heavily embroidered. The proprietor rushed forward to greet the older lady with great respect and Helena with inscrutable politeness, although probably she would have expected Mei Lee to have accompanied her mother-in-law.

Helena saw quite a different side of her mother-in-law here, as she chatted animatedly to the staff of the establishment and admired the sumptuous fabrics. Although two new dresses had already been ordered it became clear that mother-in-law was choosing fabrics for herself and Helena, however some of them were gorgeous even if the style would probably be old-fashioned. At length a bronze-coloured silk was chosen for the older women and a bright clear turquoise for Helena. Again the business of taking measurements and choosing styles was over very quickly and Helena rather feared the finished dress would look more like a dressing gown than an evening dress, but never mind; she knew she was going to have the other two dresses.

A few days later, Helena took Gerda with her for a fitting at the first dressmaker and was delighted with the results.

"Oh, you'll be the belle of the ball," exclaimed Gerda as Helena twirled in one of the almost-completed dresses.

All three gowns were delivered on the same day in good time for the banquet. Helena hung them in her closet without showing them to Fu Yan, thinking to give him a surprise when they dressed for the banquet.

Before that day came, another milestone was approaching, for Erica had been accepted by the nuns to attend the convent school and was due to start next week. The simple uniform required was all ready for her while the school would provide writing equipment and most books, for a fee. All that remained was for Helena to somehow procure the traditional German starting school gift for Erica, as she determined that her children shouldn't lose sight of their European heritage. This was a colourful cardboard cone filled with sweets and treats. As usual, the best thing was to ask Gerda, who agreed it was a super idea but could only suggest making it herself as there was nowhere in Peking to buy such a thing. Accordingly the two friends shopped for cardboard, glue and paint and spent a fun-filled morning making the prettiest cone they could and later enjoyed filling it.

The school morning came with Erica excited in her uniform and delighted with getting a present as well. She insisted on taking it to school when Helena explained its purpose although wasn't sure what the straight-laced nuns would make of it.

For the first few days Erica trotted happily off to school, holding the hand of the servant charged to deliver her, but by the end of the week she was becoming reluctant and belligerent. Her parents thought she was probably just tired and so humoured her and arranged a restful weekend. The following week, however, was no better and Helena was very cross to receive a note from the nun who was her class teacher, complaining that Erica was being naughty in class and asking to arrange an interview. Helena knew that Fu Yan would be furious so she kept the note hidden while she decided what to do.

On the day of the banquet, Fu Yan had several important meetings so he wouldn't be home to change until quite late. Apart from caring for the baby, Helena arranged to do little else so that she could pamper herself and get ready for the party. This was not to be! Halfway through the morning the janitor from the convent hammered on the large outer door and was breathlessly shown in to see Helena.

Helena looked up from changing little Manfred.

"Can I help you?"

"The sisters sent me to bring her back."

"I don't understand."

"Your daughter, Erica, ran away from the school and the convent sisters think she came home." The man articulated each word slowly and clearly as if he thought he was addressing an idiot.

Panic gripped Helena and, seizing Manfred half-dressed in her arms, she ran to find the Amah. No-one in the house had seen the child but the servants tried to calm Helena saying what a sensible child she was and how she probably just went for a walk.

"She wouldn't do that, she knows she has to stay at school. We must find her."

Helena handed the baby to the Amah and begged the other servants to help her search. As she ran out of the house she saw her mother-in-law standing in the corner of the courtyard with a knowing look on her face.

The streets and alley ways were empty and Helena's heart was hammering in her chest when she turned a corner that led to the university. She ran on knowing she must tell Fu Yan, but also fearing to do so. Luckily he was in his office and jumped up from his desk as his wife burst in.

Helena was so breathless and distraught that it took some time to explain what had happened. As soon as Fu Yan understood what had happened he went to the door of his office and called to his secretary to arrange for a group of students and staff to form a search party. Then he tried to calm Helena and told her to go home in case Erica returned there.

Helena couldn't really remember how she got home; between the lump in her throat, the pain in her chest and the recent memory of the baby being lost, she felt as if she was in a nightmare from which she couldn't wake up.

At home she went straight to Manfred and hugged his sturdy little body to her. The Amah, too, was in great distress, wringing her hands and crying so Helena sent her for some tea to calm them both.

The day dragged in an agony of waiting but at last, mid-afternoon, a servant came running in calling that the child had been seen coming in the big gates at the front of the compound.

Helena didn't know whether to scream at her or hug her and, in the event, she did both. A messenger was immediately sent to find Fu Yan and he soon returned home. Erica expected a spanking but instead he calmly took her into his study where, in long discussions, they learnt that the girl had been feeling jealous of the baby left at home while she was sent to school where nuns did not idolise her as she had expected.

It was late afternoon by the time the problems had been soothed and Erica had promised never to run away again.

Fu Yan and Helena now had to rush to get ready for the banquet, nothing like the relaxed and pampered preparation she had planned. She just did her best to fix her face and hair and slipped on the blue dress, knowing that her husband was waiting in the hallway. A quick glance in the mirror satisfied her that the dress looked as good as she had hoped but as she went to meet Fu Yan she found her mother-in-law waiting with her usual sour look on her face.

"I thought you would wear the traditional style dress. That is too modern for such an important occasion," exclaimed her mother-in-law with a sneer.

Helena hesitated, but then steeled herself and replied "I don't have time to change, Fu Yan is waiting."

Probably she was storing up more trouble but when she saw how Fu Yan's eyes lit up at the sight of her, she knew she had made the right decision.

Chapter 9

After the banquet, at which Helena really was the belle of the ball, she expected some repercussions about her dress but none came. Indeed Mother-in-law was most amenable, coming most days to visit little Manfred and taking pleasure in jiggling him till he smiled and chuckled. Diplomatically, Helena made sure to wear the traditional style Chinese dress on the occasions when the family ate meals together.

Chatting with Gerda one afternoon in her garden while Manfred slept in his baby carriage, Helena talked about how glad she was that things had calmed down after all the dramas of the previous months.

"Yes, it must be good for you to settle into a calm routine although, with all the news that one hears in the city, we have to wonder how long Peking will be the place we know."

"What do you mean?" asked Helena.

"Well, my husband deals a lot with diplomats, as you know, and he feels that international relations are really strained. Since the Japanese went into Manchuria, he reckons the writing's on the wall for further invasion."

Helena sighed thoughtfully but made no reply as Gerda busied herself with the tea things. "Would you like tea or coffee today?"

"Oh, I'd better have tea please. Coffee seems to make me nauseous lately."

Gerda glanced sharply up at her friend and Helena nodded.

"Yes. I think I may be pregnant again."

"Oh Helena, it's too soon. What is Fu Yan thinking of?"

"Ach, it'll be fine," replied Helena airily. "After all it's so much easier here than back in Germany. Having servant's means you have so much more time."

"I know that, but look at the hard time you had with Manfred's birth."

"Dr Chapman said that the problem was almost certainly a one-off. So I'm not bothered about that and anyway we have full confidence in him."

"I'm sorry to tell you but Gene Chapman and his wife are in the process of moving to Xain," said Gerda.

"Are you sure?" asked Helena. "Why are they moving again so soon?"

"Well, it's what I was saying to you earlier: the International community is anxious about Japan's intentions in this area and the Americans have this policy of non-intervention in foreign conflicts since so many of their soldiers were killed in 14–18. So the American consulate has advised its citizens to go to safer areas because they cannot offer help or protection if there's trouble."

"How do you know all this Gerda?"

"My husband explained it to me, just yesterday actually," replied Gerda.

Helena immediately began to look despondent. "Oh dear, I really was counting on him to be around, just in case."

"Don't worry, my dear. I'm sure you're right that the complication was rare and you'll be fine this time." Gerda sought to reassure her friend and quickly changed the subject to talk about her preparations for a forthcoming visit to her husband's family in the countryside outside Peking.

"Oh," said Helena, "You are going visiting and we are getting a visit. Fu Yan's cousin from Nanking and his wife are coming for a few days. He's very happy about it because they were together a lot as lads even though Tao is a bit younger."

"It's a Chinese custom at this time of year to visit your older relations, if you can," explained Gerda.

"I didn't know that. I suppose he's mostly coming to see his aunt then but never mind it will be nice to meet them".

"Is he a teacher too?" asked Gerda.

"No I think he is some sort of Government Official, that's why he has to work in Nanking."

Manfred was beginning to stir and it would soon be time for his next feed so Helena thanked Gerda, said goodbye, and pushed the baby carriage back home, deep in thought about this renewed uncertainty in the future.

Helena was happily involved with the preparations for their visitors for she was glad to be to contribute some of the welcoming touches she had learnt at home in the Pension; small things like fresh flowers and scented herbs beside the pillow make all the difference, her Mama had always said.

On arrival Tao and his wife Su Lin were travel weary so greetings and the drinking of tea were brief before they retired to their room to rest. When they were refreshed the couple emerged from their room bearing gifts for both the children. Always proud to show off their family, Fu Yan and Helena fetched little Manfred and Erica. The baby, by this time a boisterous toddler, entranced his older cousins and happily engaged with them in playing with the toys they had bought.

Erica also played to the gallery, showing her good manners by bowing low and answering in faultless Mandarin. The gift she received was something very special; a carefully chosen set to enable her to learn the art of Chinese brush-painting in which Su Lin was very accomplished. They also explained to her that Su Lin would be happy to give her some lessons while they were staying in order to give her a good start.

By now the special welcome meal was ready so Manfred was taken to the nursery to his Amah and Fu Yan's mother joined them to preside at the head of the table. The meal was a great success and everyone enjoyed the special dishes, happy conversation and some rice wine to end with.

Helena's mother-in-law had been beaming all through the meal, delighted at being fussed over and eating more than Helena had ever seen her manage. At last the old lady and Erica went off to bed while the young people moved into the cool courtyard.

After checking on the children, Helena, too, sat down to relax with her guests. Before long the conversation turned to political matters as so often happened in Peking these days. The main concern for Tao and Su Lin seemed to be the possibility of having to move if Tao's office relocated as many people as expected. Fu Yan confirmed that the possibility of relocating the university had also been mooted on more than one occasion and he personally felt it might happen sooner rather than later.

"But, come," said Fu Yan with his most charming manner, "we have just a few days together, let's enjoy them. Tomorrow Helena and I will show you some of the sights of Peking and in the evening there is a special opera performance that I'm sure you will enjoy. My mother will come to the opera with us, too. That will be a real treat for her."

"How lovely," simpered Su Lin, "but I must set aside some time to teach Erica the basics of brush-painting."

"No problem. We have time."

The visit was a delightful interlude for Helena, who enjoyed being hostess and who spent a good deal of time conversing with Tao as Su Lin always contrived to be next to Fu Yan. As far as the brush-painting lessons went, no-one could believe how quickly Erica took to the technique and what delightful results she produced.

"She definitely has a talent for painting," said Su Lin. "She's very artistic and has a wonderful eye for colour."

All too soon, the visit came to an end and the family waved goodbye to their guests. Helena was surprised to see her mother-in-law almost in tears at the farewells but she was actually rather relieved.

During the visit she had noticed a number of times how Su Lin flattered and admired Fu Yan. Flirting was too strong a word but it still awoke in Helena the nagging doubts that were always there. Would she ever be able to really trust him?

Life settled back into its normal routine and Helena met up with Gerda in their favourite tea house to compare notes about Gerda's trip and Helena's visitors. Helena took along some of Erica's brush-painting sketches to show her friend, who was duly impressed.

"You all got on really well then?" asked Gerda.

"Well, yes, but Toa's wife was all over Fu Yan whenever she got the chance. I was beginning to get really annoyed."

"Mmm, well it's only to be expected. He's a very attractive man after all."

"Yes, but he's a married man!"

Gerda shrugged and dismissed the subject, while Helena was left wondering if she would ever understand the customs and morals of this land.

Chapter 10

By now Helena was sure of her pregnancy but apart from a bit of queasiness in the mornings she felt really well. The news about Dr Chapman leaving Peking had come as a shock but with the whole of China in so much turmoil it would be soon almost a commonplace incident. Helena visited the doctor and his wife with a small parting gift and made it just a social call, keeping off medical and political matters.

Fu Yan too had heard about the doctor's departure and commented that many foreigners were leaving Peking as though it was a sinking ship. Helena told him about the pregnancy and said she wished Dr Chapman wasn't leaving. He was delighted with the news and held her close saying reassuringly, "Everything will be fine this time. We'll find another really good doctor or nurse."

By now the harsh Peking winter was upon them and though the house had fires in most rooms and only slim windows in the thick walls, it was not easy to keep warm. Helena dressed herself and the children in several layers of the warm padded clothes that all Chinese wore in the winter. With her increasing bulk and the thick layers she had to laugh at the round and shapeless image in the mirror. She was putting on a lot of weight and put it down to the generous bowls of hot noodle soup that the cook provided to keep out the cold.

A few weeks later, true to his word, Fu Yan introduced Helena to a young Chinese midwife who had attended the wives of several important men in the city and had an excellent reputation. The two women rapidly struck up a rapport and often laughed and enjoyed each other's company on the regular check-up visits. Helena was constantly pronounced to be in excellent health and the pregnancy quite without incident. Helena regularly strolled down to the university with the children where they enjoyed running about even in the cold. The icy days and frequent snow showers reminded Helena so much of her native land.

Sometimes Gerda and her boys accompanied them and on one occasion they all joined in a lovely game of snowballs. Gerda was often busy however because she was asked to help other members of the embassy with preparations for moving as well as beginning her own packing for it was almost certain that they would soon leave Peking.

At last spring was beginning to knock at the door; there were green shoot to be seen on the campus and bird song to be heard. After one of their walks Helena was pushing the baby carriage through the great gate of the house when she was pulled up by a sharp twinge that she recognised as a practice labour contraction.

Expecting that she would have plenty of time, she continued with arranging for the children's supper and their usual evening routine. After only an hour or so, however, the contractions were rapid and strong enough for her to send for Fu Yan and the midwife. Before they arrived Helena's mother-in-law appeared carrying a small jug of some greenish liquid. This she handed to Helena, saying "This will help you." Yet again Helena was amazed that the old woman always seemed to know exactly what was going on although she rarely left her room, especially in winter. She thanked her uncertainly and took a tiny sip.

Just then the midwife arrived and began to bustle around organising things. As soon as her mother-in-law left, Helena handed the girl the drink saying, "I don't want this, please get rid of it." Their eyes met and as the nurse sniffed the jug she grunted softly; they both suspected it contained opium.

Fu Yan popped his head round the door and was assured that everything was going well, before being shooed away to wait somewhere else.

This time there were no complications and before long a lusty cry was heard and the midwife proudly announced, "You have another little boy." Helena breathed a deep sigh of relief and closed her eyes for a moment, then she thought she must have misunderstood the nurse's dialect when she heard, "There's another one."

"What do you mean?"

"There's another baby and it'll be born very soon," laughed the nurse. "Oh, I am so happy! I have never delivered twins before!"

No-one was more amazed than Helena, except perhaps Fu Yan, when he was presented with a new son and daughter, both quite small but fit and healthy. He stroked both their cheeks and kissed Helena's forehead before rising to go and tell his mother the news. Yet again the old woman's subtle but pervasive influence made itself felt, leaving Helena feeling resigned but unprepared for the next bombshell. This dropped later the next day when she called Fu Yan to help decide on the names for the twins.

His immediate response shocked the dumb-founded Helena for he said his mother wanted to choose the names for the twins and he had agreed it would be nice for her. Sensing quickly that his wife's response would be hostile, he remembered an urgent task in his office and left the house.

Anger and disappointment in equal measure made Helena tearful for a time and she felt she must vent her feelings so she sent one of her servants to Gerda's house to tell her the news about the birth, knowing that her friend would come to visit as soon as she could.

Sure enough within the hour came a tap on the door and Gerda swept in carrying gifts for babies and mother. She stopped in her tracks though when she saw Helena's gloomy face. Fearing a return of the post-natal depression she hugged her friend and enthused over the babies, making much of how lucky she was to have two such gorgeous babies.

"Come on cheer up! I bet Fu Yan's over the moon isn't he?"

"Well, yes, but do you know what he's done now?"

"No, what?" asked Gerda, dreading what she might hear.

"He's agreed that his mother can choose their names!"

"Oh, is that all? Mmm, she does like to keep control, doesn't she! But actually it's not unusual for the older generation to get involved in that way. You know it's part of the whole Chinese respect for the elders thing."

Helena sighed and pouted. "But she'll choose Chinese names that I've never heard of."

"Yes but you can usually give them pet names or change the pronunciation a bit so it's nearer to what you want. That's what we did with our second – his Chinese name is Jen Yu but we called him Eugene. Easy."

"So you have had the same thing Gerda?"

"Yes, dear, we all have and it's really not worth making yourself ill or unhappy. Come on, let's have some tea or maybe a little fizz." Just at that moment, Gerda pulled from her basket a half bottle of Russian wine that she had been saving for just such an occasion.

Returning from the university, late as usual, Fu Yan went to Helena's room with some trepidation but was glad to find her happily feeding one of the twins and seeming to have accepted the situation. In fact, with Gerda's help, she had now come to see it as another opportunity to strengthen her own position.

In the end the names chosen were Bai An (Peace) and Li Na meaning Graceful and in any case just the same as Lena, a name well known in Europe. Also Bai An could be known as Brian if he liked. Helena made it clear that she was accepting this under some sufferance and expected recompense in the form of, perhaps, gold bracelets to celebrate the twins birth. Fu Yan readily agreed, having wondered both how he could thank her for such a wonderful gift and how he could make it up to her for her mother's interference.

Helena then went on to tell him about the Russian champagne and about Gerda's invitation to them to attend the next foreign reception at the embassy. It seemed, now that Mei Lee was well out of the picture, that Peking society would welcome them, for university tutors were always well regarded. The event was not to be for a few weeks hence and Helena was glad that would give her time to regain her figure so she could wear one of her favourite gowns.

When the evening arrived they made a very handsome couple, both in elegant evening dress. Erica had enviously watched her mother getting ready for the outing and as her parents bade her goodnight she wistfully sighed, "I wish I could come too".

Fu Yan smiled but said "You re much too young yet."

"No, I'm not, I'm nearly as tall as Mama."

Helena tried to pacify her by saying, "Maybe another time dear I'll ask Gerda."

"I'll ask her myself!" retorted Erica and flounced out of the room.

The girl was feeling her feet in her teenage years and showing clear signs of becoming more rebellious.

The evening was wonderful. Helena soon forgot the little altercation at home while enjoying glamorous company, lovely music and tasty titbits of food. There was also some more of that delicious Russian champagne.

On the way home they talked about the various new acquaintances they had made and Helena was clearly hoping that the invitation would be repeated though Fu Yan was not quite sure; he enjoyed the company of his academic colleagues more than the rather too political company of the embassy.

At home, Erica was still awake and had quite forgotten her earlier tantrum. She eagerly greeted her parents and plied them with questions about who they had met, what people were wearing and the food and drink. Finally she was "shooed" off to bed where she lay thinking about the scenes that had been described to her and planning how she could become part of it.

Over the next few weeks Gerda visited often, wishing to see her friends as much as possible before she and her family had to move. She also held several parties to repay hospitality and to re-connect with her various groups of friends. Helena was invited to all of them, thus ensuring that she would have plenty of invitations in the future. Erica was invited too on several occasions after Helena had told her about the girl's wish to be included.

All too soon the day arrived for Gerda and her family to pack up the last few possessions and leave to join her husband in Chongqing. She and Helena parted sadly for their friendship had meant a great deal to them both. Sincere promises were made to keep in touch by letter although mail to and from the interior was notoriously unreliable.

"Make sure you send me some pictures of the twins too," said Gerda. "They are so adorable."

With an effort she jauntily waved and departed.

Returning sadly into the house, Helena picked up Bai An and snuggled into him, silently agreeing with Gerda that they truly were adorable. Later that same day Li Na was unusually fractious and, when Helena tried to sooth her, she found the baby felt very hot and seemed to be running a temperature. The little girl refused to feed, again very unusual, so she just gave her a drink of cooled water and put her to bed, hoping a night's sleep was what she needed.

Both babies, however, had a very restless night and so did Helena and the Amah, taking turns to nurse them and cool them with damp cloths. By the morning, Helena was sure they were sickening for something and sure enough when they were changed for their bath they both had a bright red rash developing on neck and chest. Trying not to panic, Helena ran to find Fu Yan to arrange for calling the doctor.

"The twins are sick," she cried, "we must get a doctor." Fu Yan could see how anxious she was and he responded quickly, asking her what was wrong so that the doctor could be informed. A servant was despatched immediately and both parents returned to the children to wait. Knowing that it would be a Chinese doctor and that Helena had little faith in Chinese medicine, Fu Yan tried to reassure her that childhood ailments were known to respond well to herbal remedies.

When the doctor arrived he was a young Chinese man, dressed in European style and Helena breathed a sigh of relief, thinking he would probably have more modern ideas than the older doctor. His first words were troubling, however, for he looked grave and said "I fear it maybe scarlet fever. I have seen several cases in the last few days and it seems to be spreading."

When he had examined the twins he confirmed the diagnosis and gave instructions for the other children to be kept away. Searching in his bag, he produced a pack of powder, saying, "This medicine is sometimes quite effective for children but I have to tell you the disease is more dangerous for babies."

Leaving instructions for the care of the twins and the giving of the medicine, he departed saying he would return next day. All day and into the night Fu Yan, Helena and the Amah did the best they could to comfort and nurse the twins. Soon after midnight Helena took a short rest only to be roused by the Amah, crying and saying, "She has the strawberry tongue."

"What does that mean?"

"She's getting worse."

"Call the doctor," cried Helena, scrambling off the bed and rushing to the twins' room.

It was clear the child was having difficulty breathing and her fever was still very high.

The doctor arrived very quickly and, assessing the situation, ordered them to take the little baby boy to another room. Quite soon he came out and closed the door saying "I'm sorry there was nothing I could do."

Chapter 11

With a deep sigh, Helena sat down to write a reply to Gerda's first letter from Chongqing. Her friend had sent a lovely chatty, newsy letter about settling into her new home and finding her way around a new city. Receiving that letter had cheered Helena but only briefly for the news she now had to send to Gerda was constantly at the back of her mind. Losing the little girl twin had dragged the whole household down for weeks though they tried to be grateful that they still had her brother.

Blinking back tears, she wrote all about those miserable few days and the weeks that followed. Knowing that Gerda would be distressed as well, she then wrote a long description of Bai An's recovery and his progress which was good but still the illness seemed to have put him back a bit, so that he was less robust than Manfred had been at that age.

It was delightful to see how Manfred had become his little protector, almost as though he had realised special care should be taken. The little lad of course was very precious after what had happened and everyone spoilt him whenever possible.

Not wanting her letter to Gerda to be full of misery, Helena wrote all about watching the two little boys playing together and some good news about Erica who had won a prize for her brush-painting at the convent school. Sealing the letter ready for posting, she actually found she felt better than for some time; strange how it always helps to talk to a friend, even on paper.

The children had been given their lunch of rice and egg porridge by their Amah and Manfred was playing happily with toy animals, while the baby had his nap. Helena liked them both to get some fresh air each day and decided to take them out to meet their big sister at the convent. The Amah helped her to get them ready and manoeuver the baby carriage out into the street.

Once outside, the sights and sounds of the city were all around. Passing by some market stalls, Manfred pulled on his Mama's hand to go and look at the rabbits in cages; he was also fascinated by some eels in a bucket and cast longing eyes at some sugared fruits carried by an old lady. Helena was tempted to buy some but felt unsure about how hygienic their preparation could have been, so she made the promise, "We will ask Amah to make some at home. I'm sure she knows how."

There were a few rickshaw coolies nearby to collect students who regularly rode home and one automobile with a liveried chauffer. Clearly some of the pupils were very wealthy. When Erica appeared she smiled happily to see that she was being met and she ran up to greet them, leaving the little knot of girls she was with. Her friends followed behind, lured by the fascination of a baby and were all soon exclaiming about how sweet the two little boys were.

On the way home, Erica chattered non-stop about her lessons, the sisters and a lot of the time about her friend Sonia; they were apparently now 'best friends' and planned to spend all their free time together.

At home the regular evening routine went smoothly, apart from some reluctance on Erica's part to complete her homework tasks.

"Sonia's mother doesn't make her do so much at home," pouted Erica. "She's allowed to play music and billiards with her brothers."

"Yes, well your brothers are too small yet and if she plays music, no doubt she has to practice."

Much later, as usual, Fu Yan returned from the university in a sombre mood, but was soon cheered by Erica's infectiously enthusiastic chatter. Helena suspected correctly that there had been more meetings and discussions about the future of the Faculty and the likelihood of transferring some or all of the departments to the interior. The house in Peking had been in Fu Yan's family for five generations, each one adding to it, until by current standards it was considered quite grand.

So he was understandably reluctant to leave it and as things stood, politically and economically, there was no hope of selling it.

Next day Erica ran home from school, very excited because Sonia had invited her to tea on their next free day. That day arrived the following week and Erica couldn't have been more excited if she was going to tea with the Emperor. She changed her dress four or five times, spent hours arranging her hair just so and then sat gazing out of the window waiting for the rickshaw to collect her. At last it drew up to the door but Helena would not let her get in until she had checked the address that the man was taking her to and impressed upon Erica not to be too late returning.

"Yes, yes Mama. I know, I know," the girl repeated, anxious to be off.

Of course Fu Yan and Helena were glad that Erica was making friends and would soon have a social life of her own. When Erica returned she was full of news about the tea they had eaten and the games they had played, including some with Sonia's brothers. The visit was returned the following week and Sonia proved to be a most charming and delightful girl. She and Erica spent hours chatting and practising brush-painting techniques.

"Oh, Erica, you're so much better at this than I am. I wish I had your skill," Sonia was heard to complain.

"I had a very good teacher when I first started and she did say I had a very good eye for it, but I'm sure I can help you if we practice some more."

"I'd love that, please bring your things next time you come over."

So their friendship progressed, the girls spending almost all their free time together, either in painting or discussing fashions and beauty. Erica began to be dissatisfied with most of the dresses in her wardrobe because Sonia, admittedly, did have some more grown-up styles. It wasn't long before Erica's broad hints and occasional tantrums persuaded Helena that some new dresses probably were needed

"Do you want to ask Sonia where she has her dresses made or do you want to come to my dressmaker?" asked Helena one morning at breakfast.

Erica's head shot up, "What? Am I allowed some new dresses?"

"Yes, it's true the ones you have are really becoming a little too small anyway"

Erica was now actually a little taller than her mother and her figure was blossoming.

After a moment's thought Erica dashed round the table and hugged her mother, saying "Thank you, thank you," then danced back round the table to her place, much to the delight of her two little brothers who laughed and clapped their chubby hands.

"Well, which dressmaker do you choose?" asked Helena.

"Oh, Mama, yours; your dresses are always so elegant."

Helena was actually amazed, but delighted. She had thought that Sonia as "flavour of the moment," would definitely have more sway.

"When can we go?"

"At the weekend, I will make an appointment – ok?"

Erica needed to leave for school and as she rushed off she was beaming.

Visiting the dressmaker, as always was a pleasure. Since she had been introduced by Gerda, Helena always had a most cordial reception and the designer was clearly delighted to have a younger lady to work on. At first the fabrics shown seemed to be too elaborate and Helena rejected them, even though Erica sighed and grimaced. It was clear that they needed to look at some more modern and younger styles.

"She's not quite fifteen," Helena explained. "So her styles should be fresher."

"Ah," the woman seemed to understand and in a few minutes, produced some delightful ideas, both sophisticated and demure.

Four dresses were ordered, two for daytime and two for evening.

Erica was delighted and couldn't wait for the fitting session that would be in a week or so. On the way back home, the rapport between mother and daughter was almost as that between friends. Erica chattered on about Sonia and the brush-painting lessons and also about ideas she had to help the nuns in the convent, both with the younger girls and in the library.

Erica went alone to the fitting session because Helena had to take the baby for a check-up. When the dresses were delivered, they were all pronounced to be gorgeous.

"I can't wait to show Sonia," Erica cried dancing round the room holding a slim, stylish apricot silk Cheongsam up to her body. "And wait till I show Papa how grown-up I look!"

Later that evening when Fu Yan returned from the university, Erica put on her 'fashion show' and her father was indeed enchanted to see what a lovely young woman she had become.

"What a change from the little girl I met at the train station," Fu Yan laughed. "However grown-up you become I will always remember you like that." He leant back in his chair and sighed wistfully, not at all like him really.

Helena woke in the night hearing some strange rumblings. These days she was always alert to any sounds from their younger son in case he should be unwell in the night. He had actually recovered quite well from the earlier illness but having lost a child there was always a slight worry at the back of their minds. At first the noise seemed to come from outside in the street and Helena decided to wake Fu Yan but he was already wide awake and as soon as she spoke he said, "I think that's gunfire but it's not near enough to be in the city. Go back to bed and we'll find out in the morning."

Fu Yan didn't even wait for breakfast but was out at first light, to find the city buzzing with the news of a Japanese attack at nearby Marco Polo Bridge.

Apparently the small garrison there of about a hundred men had been virtually wiped out by the surprise attack by a much larger Japanese force. The area was now under Japanese control and rumours were rife that Peking was next in the invaders' sights.

In the house too, the servants performed their tasks distractedly, stopping every now and then to listen or to argue among themselves about what might happen next.

Helena wasn't really surprised to see Fu Yan back the earliest he'd ever been. This new development in the conflict meant they must leave for Chongqing as soon as possible. Although the move was a daunting prospect, Helena comforted herself with the thought of seeing Gerda again and knowing that she would help them to find a place and settle in.

Most of the servants were to be dismissed. Just leaving enough to keep the house secure and care for the old lady who had elected to stay, refusing to be driven from her home of more than 50 years.

One further dilemma had to be settled: whether to take Erica with them and have to find a new school or let her stay at the convent where she was doing so well and was so happy. In recent weeks she had been there most of the time, helping the nuns and improving her brush-painting skills. After a lot of discussion they decided to put the facts to Erica and see if she would be happy to stay.

No contest as for as Erica was concerned.

"I must stay, the final examinations are so close. Please let me stay, I'll be alright with Nai Nai!"

Chapter 12

As they approached Chongqing at last, Helena was charmed by the view of the city: the ancient fortress walls glowed red in the setting sun, the river glinted peacefully and the cliffs behind the city seemed to shelter and guard the area, giving her the feeling of a safe haven for her family. She pointed out the ships on the river to the little boys and promised them a ride on one someday soon.

Fu Yan wanted to go straight away to the university accommodation but Helena suspected he would probably be involved in meetings for hours on end so she insisted that they go first to Gerda's where she and the boys could at least rest for a while. It wasn't difficult to find Gerda's house, it being near to the area where all the foreign embassies had been set up, and as they drew up, the door flew open and Gerda ran to meet them.

"Oh, Helena, it's so wonderful to see you. How was the journey?"

"Not bad, but rather long and tiring. You look so well – it's so good to be here."

Arm in arm like sisters the two women gathered up the children and waved Fu Yan off to complete the arrangements for their accommodation. Gerda quickly produced tea and German – style fruit cake to refresh her guest. The boys' eyes lit up and Helena exclaimed, "Oh you can get German cake here."

"Yes, it's easy to get quite a lot of foreign things because all the embassies are here and goods come in by river to the port."

"The German Embassy is particularly well set up by the way, and I was thinking we could go and see about getting you a new passport. In these uncertain days you never know when you might need it."

"Do you think that's possible?"

"Certainly, you can tell them it got lost in the move. I'm sure it'll be no problem."

The boys played and were entertained by Gerda's sons while the friends had a long catch-up chat, Helena explaining the circumstances that led to the decision to leave Erica with her Grandmother and Gerda offering lots of advice on settling in.

"I must say I like it here in general and there's plenty to do. Now the Allies have set up a Headquarters here we will get plenty of invites from naval and military sections. The downside of Chongqing, however, is the mosquitoes – you need nets for your beds – and the water situation; all the water is carried by coolies up from the river in endless chains all day long so you have to be careful how you use it really."

Fu Yan was still not back and both boys were clearly very tired so Gerda suggested putting them to bed in one of the spare rooms.

Helena was not really surprised he hadn't yet returned but she was beginning to wonder if there was some problem with the house they had been allocated. Gerda reassured her by saying that the area where the university had relocated was one of the nicest in the city and she brought out some sweet German wine to sustain them while they waited.

At last Fu Yan returned, panting and perspiring, not looking at all like his usual calm, controlled self. He sank into the nearest chair and closed his eyes.

"What the matter?" asked Helena "Is there a problem with house?"

"No the house is fine. I just need to rest for a moment."

Gerda immediately produced a special calming tea and in minutes Fu Yan was explaining how he'd been busy hiring servants.

"The house is quite large so we'll need more help and we need some water coolies. Do you know about the water situation here?"

"Yes, Gerda told me and about the mosquitoes," replied Helena.

"I suppose we'll get used to it," sighed Fu Yan.

As it was already late and Fu Yan was clearly exhausted, Gerda suggested they stay the night and visit the house in the morning. Helena expected Fu Yan to refuse politely but in fact he accepted gratefully, with one of his courtly bows that had so charmed her parents all those years ago.

Although she was dog-tired too, Helena lay awake in Gerda's guest room for a long time. She couldn't help wondering what problems they would meet at the new house and worrying about how Erica was getting on back in Peking.

Next morning, though, everything seemed brighter: the house was larger than she had thought, pleasantly airy and strongly built. There was also a fair sized garden which looked out over the river where the mighty Yangtze and Jialing merged.

Gerda was again an invaluable friend in the settling-in period, helping Helena to locate and arrange the best mosquito-nets and incense burners to discourage the insects. Most of the day to day marketing was done by the servants but Gerda knew where to find things that were slightly different, slightly special. She helped select a little school for Manfred, who was to start attending mornings only and true to her word she ensured that invitations began to arrive.

The matter of finding a new Amah for the boys wasn't so easily settled for neither Fu Yan nor Helena were happy with the very young girls who applied for the position because none of them had any real experience except looking after younger siblings. Helena began to wish they hadn't left the Peking Amah behind but she hadn't been happy to leave the city where her family were and they were glad that Erica would keep her support as personal servant and friend.

At last Gerda mentioned another friend of hers, Lisa whose Amah had a sister who was looking for a job. Apparently this woman had worked as Amah to the family of the French Ambassador but he had sent his wife and children back in Paris, believing that they would be safer there. Lisa kindly brought the woman to meet Helena and they chatted over tea and fruit.

To Helena's relief she seemed to be almost a twin to the one they left behind in Peking, similarly modest and cheerful but with sensible traditional ideas and values. Helena engaged her on the spot, not waiting for her husband's approval and not wanting her to be snapped up by someone else.

When she moved in and met the boys it was clear the choice was a good one. She was firm but gentle with her new charges and they quickly came to love her fun-loving nature while knowing they couldn't misbehave.

Now that the children were being well cared for, Helena was glad to be able to accept invitations to lunch and cocktails from new friends and the social circle of Chongqing. At first Fu Yan accompanied her to embassy functions but soon the demands of setting up the administration for the university meant that he was rarely at home and always feeling exhausted when he was. Helena's refusal to turn down invitations caused several rows but eventually he accepted that since she always went with Gerda or other girlfriends she was adequately chaperoned.

The first invitation to attend a reception on one of the American ships in the port was a cause of great excitement to Helena and her small group of friends. They were to be the guests of the captain and meet his officers. Most of the girls would be with their husbands but not all. Gerda and Helena spent the previous afternoon ironing their best dresses and having their hair done. It was fun to be able to pretend that the Japanese and the troubles were far away.

In order to reach the ship a small boat was sent for the guests, a few at a time and as Helena took the hand of a sailor to embark she remembered outings on the River Spree with her parents as a child and later with Fu Yan as a lover. Once on deck where the party was held, as it was a balmy evening, she again wished he was with her to be part of the glittering occasion. All the ladies were dressed in their best gowns while the officers shone in their uniforms and other gentlemen wore either evening dress or traditional Chinese gowns. She sighed remembering how handsome he had looked in evening dress but now the work and worry really seemed to be taking its toll on him.

Her thoughts were far away for a moment but she was brought back to the present by hearing her name.

"Good evening, Helena. I'm so glad to see you."

She turned and saw it was Gene Chapman, greeting her with a broad smile. They talked for a time, exchanging news with her and Gerda before he introduced the young American officer he was with.

James Baker took Gerda's hand, then Helena's, and bowed politely. He was very tall and extremely good-looking in that clean cut American way. Was she mistaken or did he hold her hand and her eyes a moment or two longer than was necessary?

Cocktails and canapes were being served; the naval chef had surpassed himself to present a huge variety of mouth-watering little delicacies. Further along the deck a small ensemble struck up dance music and couples were taking to the floor. Helena enjoyed the evening immensely, chatting to lots of people, making several new acquaintances and tasting new flavours. The evening was almost at an end and her feet were rather sore so she sat down near the dance floor sipping a last glass of wine. It was then that Lieutenant Baker approached her, smiling, and asked if she would like to dance.

Helena hesitated for a moment but then accepted and took his hand. How pleasant to be held gently in the arms of this young tall man. She really enjoyed the dance and was quite sorry when the music stopped and James departed, thanking her very sweetly.

On the way home the girls gossiped and laughed about the lovely time they had had.

"Well, Lieutenant Baker certainly fell for you," whispered Gerda.

"What do you mean? We just had a dance."

"I saw the way he looked at you and he couldn't take his eyes off you!"

The official news from Peking was not good, for the Japanese were advancing everywhere but for the time being Chongqing was peaceful and inclined to be very lively, while keeping aware of the uncertain future. The skeleton staff remaining in the Peking University sent Fu Yan regular bulletins and occasionally included notes from Erica and some cryptic comments dictated by her grandma. From these they learnt conflicting news that Erica was (according to her) studying hard while (according to the old lady) was always out and home late. Fu Yan decided he ought to make a visit back to Peking to put their minds at rest and accordingly began to make the arrangements.

Lieutenant Baker did not appear at any of the social functions that Helena attended in the next few weeks. She had mixed feelings about his absence for he had been most charming but she kept remembering the frisson between them when they danced. Then quite unexpectedly she glimpsed him buying fruit at a stall in the market. He must have felt her eyes on him for he looked over immediately and smiled and waved, leaving the stall at once to come to meet her. Taking her hand with old-fashioned courtesy he murmured, "I hoped I would see you again. May I invite you for a drink or a cup of tea, if you have time?"

Helena knew she should refuse, but she didn't. They talked for hours in one of the smart cafes that had grown up in the city. James walked her home and when they said goodbye he held her hand much too long.

In the following weeks, with Fu Yan away in Peking, their relationship blossomed and they were both inevitably sad when the orders were received that his ship was to sail next day.

As luck would have it Fu Yan returned just as Helena was getting ready to go to the port to wave the ship goodbye, so James sailed believing she cared little for him after all.

Fu Yan was totally exhausted after his trip and went straight to bed but not before putting Helena's mind at rest about Erica, who he had found to be in good spirits and very happy with her new friends.

The nuns, too, were pleased with her progress and her sunny nature, though apparently she did not always abide by the rules of the convent. The news about his mother was not so good; her Chinese physician had explained that she had had a few minor strokes and was often wandering in her mind. Fu Yan feared she would not live much longer.

Regarding Lieutenant Baker, nothing could be further from the truth: during the few short weeks she had known James and in the stolen moments of their intimacy Helena had found that most precious feeling of being valued as the most important person in someone's life. It was many years since she had that feeling from Fu Yan.

Helena and Gerda had a regular weekly meeting at their favourite tea house, overlooking the port, sometimes alone sometimes with other friends. A few weeks later as they sat sipping tea from the delicate china bowls, Helena asked, "I have to make an appointment with Gene Chapman in his professional capacity. Will you come with me?"

"Of course," replied Gerda, "are you ill?"

"No, I'm pregnant again."

Gerda, who could be the soul of discretion, just nodded.

Chapter 13

The clerk at the German Embassy was being exceptionally uncooperative. This was the fourth time Helena and Gerda had been to the embassy to apply for a new passport for Helena but each time either the official they needed to see was unavailable or it was the wrong day for that business. Now the officious little man, having heard their explanation and asking many questions, some quite impertinent, was shuffling papers and sniffing loudly. Finally he rose from his desk and left the room, leaving the two friends looking at each other in exasperation. At least there were some free chairs to sit on so they sat to wait, hoping there would be some further developments.

"I really didn't think it would be so difficult to get your passport replaced," said Gerda, "maybe it's not worth all the effort."

"Oh, yes it is", replied Helena, "You have no idea how important this is to me."

After a wait of almost an hour a more senior official appeared and called Helena to his desk. Then the questions began all over again, substantially the same as she had answered earlier. In the end he smiled thinly and produced a large four-page form which had to be completed.

Helena reached into her handbag for her pen but he shook his head and said "Oh no, take it away and bring it back on Thursday. That's when we deal with such matters."

Helena opened her mouth to say that she could fill it in now and leave it with them but he rose and walked smartly away before she could say anything. She let out a deep sigh instead.

"Well we made some progress anyway," said Gerda. "At least we've got the form now."

"Mmm, can I come to complete it at your house? I don't want Fu Yan to see it."

"Yes we can do that tomorrow if you like."

As it happened the completion of the passport application was considerably delayed for next morning Bai An woke with eyes so sticky they were glued tight shut and he'd a raging temperature. His Amah helped to bathe his eyes and release them while Helena rocked him to try and pacify him. When his eyes were clear he was still sobbing and very hot. He was persuaded to eat a little rice porridge for breakfast but was promptly sick so Helena immediately decided to send a message to Gerda that she had to stay at home to care for him; the Amah was quite capable of nursing him but after losing his sister Helena was always reluctant to take any chances with him. The fever persisted for two to three days and they were on the point of sending for a doctor when the young Amah came into the sitting room, beaming with the news that he was sleeping calmly and the fever had broken. Nevertheless it was a few days before he regained his strength enough to play with Manfred.

The passport form had been quite forgotten during this minor crisis and it still had to be postponed because fate had yet another card to play. This time it was a message from Peking to say that Fu Yan's mother had died. Although it wasn't unexpected, the news still came as a shock. In his responsibility for his work Fu Yan was loathe to leave the university again to make the long and arduous trip to Peking but his duty as a son had to come first. He worried a great deal about all the tasks he was neglecting and how the complex and time-consuming funeral traditions could be arranged. The answer was they couldn't; in wartime many compromises have to be made.

Helena tried her best to support him in his preparations for the journey but he was short-tempered with her and furious when she said she didn't feel she could leave the children to accompany him. It was hard to understand why this was regarded as such an important event while their baby daughter's funeral, although sad, had been very quiet.

Gerda called in to offer her condolences, having heard the news on the grapevine. She helped Helena to understand Fu Yan's attitude by reminding her that in Chinese culture respect for elders is a corner-stone of life and she suggested that he would probably be quite happy if she volunteered to take the children to the Arhat Buddhist temple to offer prayers for his mother.

"Oh, I think the boys are too young," said Helena, "they wouldn't understand, but I'd be happy enough to go myself. I've seen that temple from the outside – it looks wonderful."

When her husband returned home she put the plan to him and he was indeed pleased by the idea. As he finished packing, he explained that she should go early in the morning and be sure to wear sombre clothes and no jewellery as would be appropriate for a funeral. This plan seemed to comfort him considerably and he finally departed on the trip in a better frame of mind and with loving goodbyes to his little family. They waved him off from the gateway, Helena trying to look cheerful but noting again how suddenly he seemed to be looking so tired and much older.

Fu Yan was away for a few weeks. There was so much to do in Peking: as well as organising the funeral he arranged for the house to be shut up as he didn't feel it would be safe for Erica to live there with only servants. She was to become a boarding student at the convent until such time as she could attend university. His daughter was not happy about this and there were tears, tantrums and lots of discussions until problems were finally resolved. In the end Erica was content that she would have a good deal of freedom, her own little study area and an increased allowance.

Back in Chongqing Helena kept her promise, going with Gerda to the beautiful temple, taking offerings as expected and absorbing the calm that seemed to pour out from the walls and the many impressive statues.

"What a beautiful place," marvelled Helena. "It's so huge and all the work that went into the carvings and statues."

"It is rather fantastic, isn't it?" As you can imagine, it is very important to the Buddhist in the whole area."

The two friends then strolled in the garden area and sat for a while in the peace and quiet.

"Do you think Fu Yan will be back from Peking soon?" asked Gerda.

"Oh, I do hope so. I know he felt there was a lot do and I do hope he finds Erica is still ok."

"I'm sure she will be fine. She's a survivor that one. Maybe she'll come back with him."

"Mmm, I doubt it, she seemed determined to stay when we left."

Gerda then turned to her friend and suggested, "As we've got some more time today, shall we go back to my house and fill in those passport forms?" Maybe we could even get them to the embassy today as well".

"Oh that's such a good idea. I almost forgot about it in all the problems of the last few weeks, but I do want to get it done. Let's go!"

The form didn't take long and they were soon pushing open the heavy doors of the German Embassy again. A different face was behind the reception desk this time and Helena's spirits rose as the young man looked much more approachable. He was fresh faced, with a military bearing and a ready smile. The women produced the almost-complete form and explained the situation one more time. His first words were, "Thank goodness you are German. I've been dealing with foreigners all day and my language skills have been sorely tried. Would you like to take a seat while I check the form through and then we can go from there?"

A short time later he called them over and explained one or two of the notes which had caused Helena to leave gaps in the information. It was not difficult to fill them in when Helena understood what was required.

"I see you are from Berlin. I am too and I must say I really do miss dear old Berlin."

"Sometimes I think I shall never see it again," sighed Helena.

They then fell into reminiscing about their favourite sights and places until Gerda politely reminded her that the time was getting on and both were expected home.

"I am so sorry to delay you, Frau Yang, but it has been a pleasure talking to you. The processing of your new passport will take a few weeks but we will contact you when there is some news."

"Thank you so much. Auf Wiedersehen."

As soon as Helena reached the gate of the house, Manfred came running out crying, "Vati's home, Vati's home!" She hurried in expecting to find him at his desk as usual but instead Fu Yan was slumped in an easy chair in the living room looking exhausted and quite grey in the face but tenderly holding Bai An on his knee and a story book in the other hand.

He looked up and smiled wanly as she entered but made no attempt to move. Helena bent to kiss his forehead and felt how clammy his skin was.

"It's good to see you home but you certainly look as if you need a rest." So saying, Helena called the young Amah to collect the children and then helped her husband to his bedroom, where he laid down without protest.

The journey and the stress of his mother's death, together with all the efforts involved in arranging the funeral and other matters in Peking had really worn Fu Yan out. He slept like a man in a coma right round the clock but woke feeling only slightly refreshed. He was anxious to get back to the university, feeling that he had already been away long enough, but when he tried to get dressed he collapsed.

"Let me call Dr Chapman." Helena begged, and at first he nodded but then said: "Wait, it's better if I see a Chinese doctor, not a foreigner. My colleagues at the university would expect it."

Helena didn't see how his colleagues at the university would know either way but she agreed and sent for a well known Chinese physician who worked near to the new university offices.

The doctor arrived without delay and Helena showed him into the bedroom; he didn't look so ancient as the one who attended Helena in Peking, but not far off it. He carried nothing and walked with his hands deep in his voluminous sleeves. After greeting Fu Yan with a bow he regarded him gravely and then looked expectantly at Helena.

"You'd better wait outside, my dear," said Fu Yan.

"Oh yes, of course," replied Helena and she departed to the adjoining room.

After a long time, the doctor came out and handed her a bag of greenish powder, presumably extracted from those massive pockets in his sleeves.

"Give him this tea three times," instructed the old man "I will return this evening."

After showing the physician out, Helena went to the kitchen to make the tea and took it to Fu Yan.

"What did he say?" she asked.

"He thinks I have too much blood and the liver needs purging so he will come back with leeches."

Helena was horrified. She had seen leeches sometimes on stalls in the market and found them revolting.

At sunset the doctor returned carrying a little jar of writhing creatures, which he showed to Manfred and Bai An. They were fascinated but Helena called them away to get ready for bed while she herself kept well away from them.

That night Fu Yan again slept deeply but his breathing seemed easier and his colour was better. First thing in the morning the doctor was back with a new set of leeches and this time he took the boys into their father's room to watch.

Squeals and giggles emanated from the bedroom and the boys came rushing out to tell her what was happening. She really didn't want to know and was glad when the physician left this time, saying that Fu Yan should rest and would soon recover.

Sure enough, after a few days Fu Yan felt much better and was eager to return to work. Before that, though they managed a little time to talk over the situation in Peking. Relaxing together for a short time after their lunch on the veranda, they talked and watched the boys at play.

"I'm glad I was able to arrange most of the funeral the way mother would have wanted it," sighed Fu Yan "Convincing Erica to leave the house was not so easy, though. I began to think that it might be better if she came back with me, but she was adamant that she must stay in Peking."

"How did she look though?" asked Helena "Is she well?"

"Oh she looks marvellous – she is a very beautiful young woman but so self- willed. I hope the nuns can cope with her."

Helena sat back and hesitated a moment before saying "I have some news too, I have been to see Dr Gene Chapman."

"You're not ill are you?" Fu Yan looked really concerned.

"No, I'm having a baby."

"Oh that is good news", said Fu Yan reaching for her hand. "Perhaps we will have another little girl."

The next few weeks were the quietest Helena had known in Chongqing; Fu Yan worked at the university each day and returned late, there were very few invitations, various ships came into port and left again quite quickly. Helena had no news of James, either good or bad. It felt as though the city was holding its breath.

Then one night, just as they were getting ready for bed, came the sound of planes, many planes. Helena and Fu Yan stopped and listened, at first unsure what it meant but as the droning became more insistent, Fu Yan cried "Get the boys to the cellars!"

Just as they got down the narrow stairway, the first blasts were heard, thankfully some distance away, this time.

Chapter 14

A few weeks earlier than expected, while Helena was playing a counting game with the children in the garden, she began to feel sharp twinges that she recognised as practice contractions for the birth. She waited another hour or so until the boys had had their lunch, suspecting that it might be a false alarm, but since the pains seemed to be getting more frequent, she called the young Amah and explained the situation. The children's nurse was to take them to Gerda's house and on the way back call at Dr Chapman's office.

As soon as they had gone, taking with them a small overnight bag so the children could stay if necessary, Helena lay down on the bed trying to keep calm and taking deep breaths to help with the pains as she remembered from before. She was glad that the young Amah returned quite quickly but she was alone, bringing a message that the doctor would call by quite soon. The young woman showed herself to be a tower of strength, efficiently organising the room and calmly supporting Helena like a sister until the doctor arrived.

Doctor Chapman examined Helena, listened to the foetal heartbeat and declared all to be well as he packed his bag and prepared to leave.

"You aren't going, are you?" Helena begged.

"Oh, you'll be fine; it's a few hours yet and you are in good hands with this young lady. Don't worry I'll be back in an hour or so."

Helena sank back on the bed, smiling weakly at her companion and wondered if she should send for her husband.

Gene Chapman did return as promised but actually only just in time to watch the young servant calmly deliver the baby girl – small but healthy.

Fu Yan was sent for then and he rushed in to find his wife already sitting up, cradling the child. He was over the moon. Having recently buried his mother, the birth of a baby daughter was a great comfort and a sign of the renewal of life. In the Chinese tradition he wished to name the little girl after her deceased grandma and Helena saw no reason to disagree.

The very next day Gerda called, bearing gifts as she had been told the news by Gene. She also had some little treats for the boys so they wouldn't feel left out.

"Oh, she's beautiful Helena," cried Gerda, "all that lovely black hair and the shape of her little mouth, just like Fu Yan's!"

There were, however, more pressing matters to discuss because the Japanese air raids had continued intermittently and a place of safety during them had become paramount. The resourceful Chinese people were in the process of setting up bomb shelters in the nearby Hongya caves and had prepared an efficient warning system. Fu Yan was insisting that Helena must take the children to the caves as everyone was sure they were the safest shelter. As for himself, there was a strong cellar in the university building in an emergency or the nearby house.

Gerda with her usual efficiency had checked out the shelters in the caves and was able to advise Helena what she would need to bring for the children when the alarm was raised. So far the raids had been relatively short-lived but there were to be facilities for sleeping and eating if necessary.

"One thing though," whispered Gerda, "the German Embassy has painted a huge swastika in the back yard to protect them from the bombing. My husband says it's because of the co-operation between Japan and Germany, so when we are in the shelters it's best to speak in Mandarin."

Fu Yan overheard this and agreed wholeheartedly: "It is true, I have heard some mutterings about foreign influences. We will need to take care."

After Gerda had gone home, the young Amah and Helena set to, to prepare two or three bags that they could easily carry to the caves with items that they and the children might need. The little boys helped and both encouraged the idea that it was an exciting game.

Not so exciting was the first time they heard the warning gongs. Out in the street there was near panic and Helena was really glad of the help and protection of her husband and servant as they made their way to the caves. It wasn't far and once inside everyone felt a little calmer. They managed to settle their little group in a relatively quiet corner and minutes later Gerda arrived with her sons who, being older were reluctant to stay with the family, wanting to be nearer to the entrance watching the action. Gerda, though, was absolutely firm that they should stay nearby.

It's amazing how quickly extraordinary events can become routine and quite soon a pattern of behaviour emerged each time the air-raid warning came. In the caves the different groups, who ordinarily would not have met or associated together, struck up a rapport and helped each other. Sometimes Fu Yan came with them to the shelter but if he was at work he would either come a bit later or stay in the cellar of the university or house.

Within the shelter Chinese children and foreign children all played together. Older children and young mums taught songs and played rhymes so that the time passed quickly. While Helena fed and cared for the baby, the two boys were happily occupied watching, or trying to join in skipping games or a version of hopscotch. When the raids went on for a long time some traders miraculously appeared with steamed buns and dried fruits to sell.

Each time they left the caves Helena, Gerda and the other women in their group were horrified to see more devastation, more homes and small businesses destroyed. Fu Yan was making plans to send his family to Xian where there had been no bombing and where his cousin was now working. Although Helena dreaded the thought of leaving her home and husband behind she was becoming increasingly terrified of the frequent raids.

When there were a few days without warnings or raids life seemed to return to normal for a while and people could hope that maybe the assault was over but it seemed that the enemy were just lulling the city into a false sense of calm before the next onslaught.

"There go the warning gongs again," sighed Helena as they rushed to gather the children, trying hard to appear calm while the hard knot of fear clutched at her stomach making her hands shake.

In the caves this time the raid went on and on, making everyone more tense and fearful than usual. Fu Yan had been working in his office when they left home and still hadn't come to join them when they saw and heard a commotion nearby from the Chinese group who had received some news from outside.

"What is it?" asked Helena when Gerda had visited the group and returned.

"There's a considerable feeling of Schadenfreude," she replied, "for the German Embassy has been bombed, swastika or no swastika and all the staff have been evacuated!"

"There goes my new passport then."

"Looks like it, I'm afraid."

Hours later the raid was still going on so most people tried to get some sleep but Helena couldn't help thinking about the 'lost' passport again. Not that she wanted to go back to Germany at the present time but maybe in the future?"

At last the bombing stopped and some calm descended on the caves, tempered with anxiety for what might be found outside. This had been the worst so far.

Gradually people began to gather their things together ready to leave when the 'All Clear' sounded. Helena and Gerda were among the last to leave as the baby had started fussing just at that time and really needed feeding. As they made their way to the cave entrance Gerda's husband came up to them, looking very serious.

"Helena had better come back with us," he whispered to his wife. "There's been a lot of damage near to the university. They can't go back there at the moment."

Gerda nodded and immediately took her friend by the arm, saying "We'd like you to come back with us until the streets are a bit clearer."

She'd never said this before so Helena was immediately on her guard.

"Fu Yan will wonder where we are," she said.

"He'll probably guess," said Gerda, taking the two little boys by the hand and bustling off.

At Gerda's house a meal was prepared with the meagre provisions available; gone were the days of sumptuous foreign delicacies. Everyone was hungry so they ate but in sombre silence.

"When are we going home?" asked Manfred, sensing that something was wrong.

"Oh, quite soon darling," replied Helena. "Eat up your soup."

A few minutes later Gerda's head servant showed a tall dark visitor into the room; Helena knew he was the military attaché from the embassy. He stood to attention and after nodding to Gerda he addressed Helena.

"I'm so sorry Madam, the Dean's house near to the university took a direct hit – there was nothing we could do."

Helena gasped and somehow asked, "Was Fu Yan there?"

"Yes," He answered, shaking his head sadly. "I'm really sorry, they were in the cellar but it was not strong enough."

Chapter 15

Gerda knew her friend was in shock: She hadn't wept, she'd hardly spoken, just held the children close and stared into space. After a time she gently pulled the stricken woman to a sofa and sat holding her hands, talking gently in as reassuring a way as possible. Gradually Helena seemed to gain some realisation; she began to shake and silent tears poured down her face. Gerda's sons, at a sign from their mother, had already taken the little boys away to play with them and in a great rush all Helena's hopes, fears and guilt came pouring out.

"Oh Gerda, what am I going to do? Why didn't I make him come to the caves?"

"You couldn't have known, Helena," soothed Gerda. Then the tears really came, pouring down her face and great racking sobs.

"Oh Gerda, I did love him; I thought I'd never forgive him for what he did but in the end it didn't matter."

Gerda held her friend and rocked her until the first paroxysm subsided and her breathing grew quieter, then taking her hand she led her to a spare room and said, "Lie down while I get you a drink."

In a very few minutes Gerda was back with a sweetened camomile tea into which she had put a little Laudanum.

"Here, this will help you sleep."

Helena drank the tea, not believing that she could possibly sleep but in fact, due to the drug, she did quite quickly. Her sleep at first was deep and dreamless but after an hour or two became fitful and disturbed by images of her husband calmly walking in to see her.

She awoke when it was still dark and for a moment felt totally disoriented until the memory returned and a panic gripped her that she didn't know where the children were. She rushed out into the darkened quiet house, looking for them and calling out to them until a servant found her and led her to the room next door to where she had been sleeping. The little boys were lying fast asleep but the baby was awake and Helena was amazed that she wasn't crying, even though she must have been hungry. She gathered up the little girl and gently stroked the boys to reassure herself that they were safe.

There was little more sleep that night while Helena kept the baby close to her for comfort, part of her mind refusing to face the truth, part of her mind just numb.

In the morning Gerda, coming in with a light breakfast tray, was glad to see her friend looking calmer but still infinitely sad.

"Oh Gerda, thank you, you have been so good to me," said Helena, struggling not to burst into tears again.

"No we're just glad to help you," replied Gerda. "My husband has gone over to the university grounds to find out what he can do to help salvage and secure against looting but he doesn't think there will be too much as the academics and Dean were so respected."

Helena took a deep breath and bit her lip to help her keep control; she'd had the strangest feeling that reality had been suspended but knew it would kick in as soon as she started to confront the tasks that must be addressed.

So she began: "Do you think I should go to the house and help him? There's not much of value there only some of my jewellery. Thank goodness you've looked after the gold I've put aside."

"No, wait until he comes back. We need to think about where you and the children can go for safety."

Helena just looked bewildered, not yet being able to come to terms with this massive upheaval in her life.

"Of course you can stay here for the time being," said Gerda, "but we don't know what will happen later."

Just then the baby started fidgeting and from the kitchen the boys could be heard bickering over breakfast, so the discussion was shelved until later. The immediate problem was to keep life as normal as possible for the children.

Gerda's husband did not return for a very long time, so, becoming anxious, she sent her eldest son to find out what had happened. He returned very soon saying, "I met Papa just at the corner. He said to tell you that although the house is not habitable, some personal things are safe and will be sent over in a trunk. He can't come home yet, though, he's been called to the consulate."

By evening he had still not returned and after putting the children to bed, the friends resumed their conversation from the morning.

"I've been thinking," said Helena, "two things really. Firstly I have to inform Fu Yan's relatives and secondly maybe we could stay with his cousin in Xian, you remember the one who came to stay with us in Peking?"

"Yes, that might be in good solution. You got on quite well with them didn't you!"

"It seems a lot to ask but I haven't really any choice," sighed Helena.

Eventually Gerda's husband returned home and sank wearily into a chair while his wife quickly heated some rice and pickled vegetables and Helena made some tea.

After his refreshment he sat back and began to explain all the events of the day. It transpired that several of the other academic staff had been with Fu Yan in the shelter but none had survived; the university was in deep shock and had been making plans for a joint memorial service and a Requiem Mass but the latest development in the Japanese conflict had probably precluded that.

"Why, what has happened?" asked Helena, tearful again at the news.

"I was called to the consulate because there is Intelligence that the Japanese intend to intensify their assault on Chongqing in the near future.

They are determined to take the city so plans are underway for a mass evacuation of all who can leave."

Both women were aghast and sat in silence for a moment trying to take in what this was going to mean for them and their families. Gerda was first to recover saying "Where will we go?"

"I have been posted to Canton. The flight will be in a few days – we must prepare immediately."

His eyes then fell, questioningly, on Helena who bit her lip and said, "We have been wondering if the children and I could stay with Fu Yan's cousin Kai in Xian but he doesn't even know he's gone yet. I don't even know how I can get in touch."

"Have you got an address?"

"Fu Yan had that kind of things in an address book for sending his New Year greetings and such like."

"If it was in his desk, it's probably in the trunk. We'll look when it arrives."

"Even if we do find it, I'm not sure we can stay with them. Maybe they won't want us there," said Helena with a sigh and a worried frown.

"Oh, that won't be the case, I can assure you, my dear. In Chinese culture it is unthinkable to refuse to help family, especially when your husband was such an eminent man."

In the middle of the night Helena awoke with a shock realising that she hadn't let Erica know about the loss of her father. Another wave of guilt swept over her and she immediately got up and dressed quickly to find pen and paper. Sitting in the kitchen so as not to disturb the house, she tearfully composed the letter including the information they had just learnt about the evacuation because she knew that Erica's instant reaction would be to come to Chongqing. It took her a long time to compose the letter, stopping every now and then to remember incidents from Erica's childhood and adolescence when she and her father had laughed or quarrelled, but mostly laughed. By now it was too late to go back to sleep so Helena began to unpack the salvaged items from her trunk. After emptying about half of it she stopped and made some jasmine tea, and was warming her hands on the bowl when Gerda came in yawning and gave her a hug.

"You're up early dear," she said.

"So are you. Couldn't you sleep either?"

"Actually I got up to search for some fabric that we could use to make you a type of money belt to carry your gold around your body. You can't possibly carry it in your luggage – it would be much too dangerous."

"Oh Gerda," said Helena, "you think of everything. What will I do without you? You're going to Canton and we to Xian – I'm going to miss you so much."

"Me too, but we'll keep in touch somehow and I'm sure we'll meet again when things calm down."

The children, the stitching and desultory preparations for leaving kept the women busy all day and they were somewhat surprised when a servant announced an important visitor. It turned out to be Madame Chiang, who was on the Governing Board of the University. Helena had never met her before but had heard much about her influence in the Nationalist Movement and her humanitarian work.

Gerda quickly ordered tea and showed her visitor to the best room. She insisted though that they should not make any fuss saying; "I have called to offer this dear lady my sincere condolences and to assure her of support from the university if at all possible. Your husband was such a charming man, my dear, and he was so highly thought of by all who worked with him."

"Thank you, that's very kind," replied Helena, wringing her hands nervously.

Madam Chiang then asked Helena about her plans for the future and nodded when she heard that they would probably stay in Xian at least for a time.

The preparations for the evacuation got underway very quickly – a measure of how serious the military judged the situation to be. Gerda's flight to Canton was to be the very next day.

Unbeknown to the women, Gerda's husband had been struggling to find passage to Xian for Helena because no flights were going that way but the visit of Madam Chiang gave him an idea and idea and indeed he was able to secure places for them on an overland convoy partly arranged by the university.

All too soon the time to say goodbye arrived and Gerda, seeking out her friend, found her in tears beside the small cases which were all they could take on the truck.

"What's the matter Helena? Don't cry! You'll be alright when you get to Xian – they'll look after you."

"Oh Gerda, I'm crying because I just had to tell the boys that they won't see their father again and do you know what Manfred said?" she sighed deeply, while Gerda shook her head. "He said: It's alright Mama we'll look after you now."

Both women dissolved into tears for the sorrow of their loss and the parting.

It had been arranged that one of the servants would help Helena and the children to the meeting place of the convoy and he was kind enough to carry the smallest boy and help her onto the truck. As it pulled away Helena reflected how she had arrived in China, apprehensive but excited, and now was leaving this city as a refugee.

Chapter 16

As the truck bumped and rattled along the dusty roads on the way to Xian, Helena hoped and prayed that her letter to Tao and Su Lin had arrived safely and that there would be someone there to meet them. Gerda's husband had used all of his influence to ensure that the missive had safe passage but of course she was still concerned, having had no word back.

What good friends Gerda and her husband had been all through her time in China; Gerda had been the first friend she had made and she had helped her in so many ways. Now their paths had divided perhaps irrevocably and maybe they would never meet again. Helena had to gulp down a feeling of near panic at the thought.

Her pensive mood was interrupted by a loud wail from Bai An who suffered from travel sickness and looked as if he was about to be sick. With the truck still bowling along an elderly Chinese lady helped to clean him up and pacify him; she rummaged in her bag and gave him a small piece of a dried root to chew – it wasn't ginger but something like it and after a time it helped and he dropped off to sleep. Poor little chap, he often had tummy upsets and such like and his parents had often worried that he didn't seem to have the robust constitution of the other children.

The overnight stop at Hanzhong was just as uncomfortable as the trip; all the passengers crammed into an old timber-framed shed that wouldn't have been good enough for cattle in Germany. Two men from the group who said they knew the town went out to find food but returned empty-handed. However some message must have gone round for some locals eventually appeared with hot tea and some dumpling broth.

Helena was glad of the tea and ate a little of the broth knowing she must keep her body nourished as she was still feeding the baby.

Manfred, who always had a good appetite tucked into a bowl of broth but the younger boy wouldn't eat anything. As night fell, everyone tried to settle down to sleep with whatever comforts they had with them. The elderly couple next to Helena again were really helpful, telling the boys stories until they fell asleep and keeping them both between their bodies for warmth.

During the morning of the next day Japanese planes flew overhead and some people screamed, fearing that the convoy would be bombed, but luckily their target was obviously elsewhere, probably Chongqing.

At last the city walls of Xian came into view and the passengers began to chatter excitedly about the prospect of a decent meal, a comfortable bed or a hot bath, whichever was their priority. Some of the group were to stay with relatives like Helena, others had hopes of a job, some knew not what the future held. As the trucks negotiated the narrow streets inside the city walls, the locals looked up from their daily tasks with little interest; since the war with Japan had escalated they had frequently seen such comings and goings.

Finally the main square was reached – where the journey ended and the trucks were to be unloaded. Here the atmosphere was quite different: Helena looked out across a heaving sea of humanity composed of traders, relatives, travellers, all searching for something or someone. She was reminded with a shock of her arrival in Harbin all those years ago – everything so foreign and so frightening.

Scrambling down from the truck, trying to keep the children safe and their meagre luggage together took all of Helena's strength and effort. This busy interlude had kept her from worrying about what to do next but as the children looked up at her and around, wide-eyed, at the bustle on all sides, she began to panic. She had no idea how to get to Tao's house and was not sure they would be welcome there. People were pushing and shoving past her, stepping over the bags, intent on reaching their goals before dark.

At that moment something drew Helena to look up and her eyes met those of a young woman across the square who was frantically waving and calling "Mama!" It was Erica! She couldn't believe her eyes as her grown-up daughter battled her way across the square, clearly under the protection of a tall distinguished young man.

Tears filled both their eyes as they met and hugged, emotions warring between the joy of meeting up, and the grief that they both shared for their loss. Helena managed to speak first with the thought uppermost in her mind "How did you get here?"

"Nikolei drove us – he's a marvellous driver." Erica smiled as she touched his arm.

"Have you seen Tao then?"

"Yes, they would have come to meet you but there was not enough room in the car for everyone."

Together the three of them gathered up the children and the luggage and made their way back across the square to where a group of young lads were admiring the foreign vehicle. Nikolei shooed them off and with some difficulty, everything was piled into the car. It was only a few minutes' drive to the narrow street where Tao lived and as soon as the car drew up he came out to greet them. Inside the house Su Lin greeted them too but with noticeably less warmth.

As soon as everything was unloaded they all sat around a low table to drink tea and talk about the events that had led to their current situation, trying not to say too much about Fu Yan's death to avoid upsetting the children. Tao talked a lot about the Nationalist Movement and how the Chinese way of life would change if Mao's proposed new order came about.

After a simple meal, it was time to put the children to bed – they were to sleep in a corner of the main room and Helena was shown a tiny cubicle where she could sleep.

Of course she didn't say anything but she was quite horrified at their living conditions compared to what she had had in Peking and Chongqing; when the cousins had visited them they had certainly given a different impression but maybe wartime had reduced their circumstances too.

Nikolei had gone out on an errand as soon as he had eaten and returned with some fresh fruit and the news that he had booked a room nearby. Over the fruit, the family reminisced together about times in Peking, with many memories of Fu Yan and his mother.

Helena was really tired and quite glad when Nikolei rose to leave, thinking that now they could all go to bed. Erica, too, got up and came to say "Goodnight."

"Where are you going?" asked Helena.

"Nikolei has booked a room for us. Uncle doesn't have room for us all to stay."

"You can't do that – it's not respectable."

"Of course it is," laughed Erica. "We are married."

"You're what?"

"We've been married for nearly four months," replied Erica, taking Nikolei's hand and smiling up at him.

"But you're much too young to marry," said her mother.

"I'm nearly as old as you were."

Erica pouted defiantly and Helena sighed because she couldn't face a big row at this time and anyway it wouldn't be appropriate in someone else's house.

"We'll talk about it another time. I'm very tired now."

"Goodnight Mama." Erica gave her mother a quick hug and her son-in-law took her hand for a moment as they left.

As she fell asleep at last, Helena couldn't help wondering what Fu Yan would have thought and said if he had lived. She suspected his fury at that young man would have known no bounds.

After quite a disturbed night and all the stresses of the previous few days, Helena slept quite late and by the time she dressed, Su Lin had already given the boys their breakfast and was entertaining them by drawing simple pictures and Chinese characters. They made a laughing happy group and Helena realised she must put aside her former dislike and suspicions of the woman and be friendly and of course very grateful that they had been taken in in their hour of need. To this end, Helena helped as much as possible in the house although two women in what was actually a very small apartment and a minute kitchen was a recipe for tensions before long.

For the first few days Erica and Nikolei were also often at the house, making it even more crowded. Erica was a great favourite with Su Lin especially after making such good progress in the art of brush-painting taught to her by the older woman and they had a lot in common, chatting about pigments and techniques. Mother and daughter were rarely alone to be able to discuss the matter of her marriage and their future.

Before long, however there were hints from Nikolei about returning to Peking and Helena realised she must find an opportunity to talk to them before it was too late. Not knowing the city at all really, she had no idea where to go for some privacy, so she quietly asked Nikolei to help and he was very good, proposing a short walk and visit to a tea garden for the three of them. Su Lin was happy to look after the children so they left promising to be only an hour or so.

Nikolei discreetly left mother and daughter to talk while he wandered around the garden and ordered some tea and dumplings. To preclude an interrogation from her mother Erica immediately explained all about how she had met Nikolei at one of the embassy functions way back when the family were still in Peking. Very quickly they had fallen in love and just recently he had begged her to marry him in case he was recalled to Moscow.

"And if he is recalled to Russia, what will you do?"

"I'm not sure. I still have my work with the nuns and my studies in Peking, but we hope it won't come to that."

Helena nodded, seeing her much-loved daughter glow with

happiness in her marriage she couldn't help but be glad for her.

"You both seem very much in love and he's certainly very charming but I wish you'd waited so we could have met him first. However, what's done is done and I wish you happiness. When do you have to go back?"

"In a day or two, I'm afraid. We only got permission to leave because of Vati;"

At the mention of her father both women felt their grief and emotion strongly and wept together for a few moments regardless of their surroundings.

After the young people returned to Peking life settled into a sort of routine at the apartment but Helena was soon aware that she would need to find a way to contribute to the household budget and pay her way a bit. She did not want to start dipping into her gold reserve as that was her only security for the future. Although Su Lin had been very helpful and supportive at first, resentment was beginning to build up and there was a strange dynamic in the house whereby Tao contrived to be at home often when his wife was not and his attentions to Helena made her very uncomfortable. Whenever possible Helena, too, went out on these occasions, walking with the children to keep out of his way.

On just such a day the little family group found themselves near the main square as a convoy of military vehicles passed by. The boys excitedly waved and as the jeeps and trucks rushed by in a cloud of dust Helena caught sight of a familiar face.

Chapter 17

Nikolei had managed to obtain sufficient petrol to make the return trip to Peking but only by paying over the odds and greasing the appropriate palms. He was quite used to this sort of thing, however, for life in Peking under the Japanese occupation had remained comfortable but only if you knew where and how to obtain the luxuries that some considered necessities.

The roads on the long trip back were not very busy and much of the way was through quiet rural areas so Erica found the drive quite boring and before long she slipped into a daydream, remembering all the events that had happened since her parents had left her in Peking.

The preparations for the family to move to Chongqing went on for several days and all the while Erica had raged inwardly about having to leave her friends and the city where she was so happy.

"Well, just tell them you don't want to go!" Sonia was fed up with hearing her friend whinge and complain about moving to Chongqing.

"I can't do that. Papa will just say I'm too young. I know he will."

"Then you'll have to go, won't you!" Sonia shrugged and turned back to restyling her hair. It was the nearest the friends had come to a quarrel.

On the way home Erica scuffed in the dusty path while rehearing what to say in order to convince her parents to let her stay, but it didn't sound convincing, even to her. How amazed she was that she didn't even need her prepared speech because they left the decision to her.

She remembered waving and waving as they drove away until they were out of sight. Mama had had tears in her eyes that made Erica weepy as well and as she turned back into the house her feelings were a jumble of bewilderment and exhilaration. Her old grandmother was sitting in her usual chair, regarding her with those shrewd eyes and a knowing smile.

Judging it best to preserve her studious image, Erica gathered up her books and left for the convent. In the evening she returned at a reasonable hour, having only stopped for a short time to visit Sonia, hoping as always to also meet her friends and brothers. That fact was that, although Erica genuinely did enjoy working with the nuns and did hope to go to university, the main reason she wanted to stay in Peking was a massive crush on Sonia's eldest brother.

Back at home Erica and her grandmother shared a simple meal of soup and steamed pork buns – a favourite with them both, before companionably chatting long into the night. The old lady reminisced about Fu Yan and his exploits as a boy and as a young man, while she smoked several cigarettes, having promised him she would not smoke opium in front of Erica. Before going to bed Erica tentatively asked about the allowance that had been left for her and was delighted to hear that it was very generous indeed.

Getting ready for bed, Erica missed a good night kiss and allowed herself a little weep but soon cheered up by planning how she would spend her allowance on some more new clothes and make-up and some outings with her friends.

Every day Erica did spend some time at the convent or in the university library as she knew that was expected of her but increasingly the lure of socialising with friends caused her to find excuses to be out and about. Sonia's family appeared to have no qualms about remaining in the city and certainly no difficulty in continuing to obtain an adequate supply of quality foreign goods. Her parents were fond of the young exotic woman who was Sonia's best friend and Erica was always included in their various parties and soirees, especially as they knew that her family had fled to a ' safer ' area.

In China the most important celebrations were always the Chinese New Year but in Sonia's home they kept the American traditions more, so that Thanksgiving was important and the January New Year celebrated with lots of food, wine and dancing.

Erica had bought a beautiful new dress for the occasion, midnight blue and very sophisticated, and she'd chosen her moment carefully to tell her grandma that she'd be staying over. It was quite easy to persuade the old woman of anything if you chose the time when she was warmly ensconced in her room with the tell-tale sweet aroma of the little pipe lingering.

The party was wonderful: lots of young men asked both girls to dance and Erica was overjoyed when Sonia's eldest brother asked her to dance just as midnight approached. Then, joy of joys, as chimes rang out on a radio somewhere, he kissed her; just a peck on the cheek but it took her breath away.

Though tired she was too excited to sleep straight away and her eyes were glowing as she enthused to Sonia about the delightful evening and about being sure she was in love with her brother. Sonia said little.

In the coming days, each time the girls met Erica looked for and asked about the beloved brother but he was never around. Eventually Sonia got tired of her friends continual fruitless adoration of the boy and decided she must tell her a few home-truths.

"Erica, for goodness sake don't keep on about it. You talk as if it's a love affair – it's nothing of the sort and never will be."

"What do you mean? We always get on really well. We danced and he kissed me."

"Yes he likes you as a friend but it can't be more than that. Don't you see he could never marry a girl with a Chinese father."

Erica had felt she had been slapped in the face. It had never occurred to her that such prejudice could affect her, although she had heard the nuns talk about the problems for Eurasian orphans. Without saying a word, she left and ran all the way back to the convent.

As Sonia had feared, telling her friend the truth had driven a wedge between them; they still spoke when they met at social occasions or at the opera playhouse but their close friendship had been damaged, perhaps for ever.

Soon Erica was being courted by an eager suitor – a young man who had admired her for some time. This was Nikolei Androv, from the Russian Embassy, a talented young attaché with an eye for the girls and especially for the exotic looks of the young Eurasian girl.

Erica's first real date was when he invited her to cocktails at the Hotel de Pekin. He was charm itself, and she, dressed in her best, looking stunning, was quickly bowled over. The romance progressed rapidly with the result that Erica's grandmother rarely saw her and began to be really concerned at the late hours she was keeping.

The consequent visit by Fu Yan was a joy to Erica who had always adored her father but she kept the truth of her romance a secret, fearing that he might not approve. Now she deeply regretted that she had deceived him the last time he saw him.

At last they arrived in Peking and enjoyed driving through the city they both loved, past the Forbidden City and the old village quarter but hated seeing the Japanese patrols marching with their cruel and faceless abstraction. Nikolei dropped his wife at the convent and then drove onto the embassy to report back.

On entering the main building Erica met Father Martin the young Irish missionary who had married them a few months ago.

"Hello Erica. I heard you went to visit your mother. How is she?"

"Oh, she's well enough, thank you. She and the children are staying with relatives."

"That's good." Replied the priest and walked on by.

Erica made her way to the convent kitchen to make a cup of tea and await Nikolei's return.

Later that evening, back at their small apartment near the embassy, Erica started to unpack their luggage from the trip but Nikolei called her over:

"Come here a minute darling, I need to talk to you."

"What's the matter? Did you get into trouble for taking time off?"

"No, it's not that – I've been called back to Moscow. All the young, fit staff from the embassy have to go – only the old men remain."

Erica gasped and her heart missed a beat. She sighed and bit her lip but said nothing because in her heart of hearts she had expected it.

"When do you have to go?"

"In a few days, but listen we will make those days so special and have enough fun to last until I get back."

Erica nodded and smiled a watery smile. His exuberance and zest for life was one of the things she loved most about him – he was nothing like some of the other dour foreign diplomats she had met.

Those precious few days passed in a whirl. As Nikolei had promised they danced, they drank Champagne and they made love. All too soon the transport arrived and he was gone.

Erica had never felt so alone and although the nuns were kind she found most comfort in the time she began to spend with Father Martin. He was a good listener, a kind man and a real friend. It was useful to him as well to be able to converse with Erica because although he had worked hard to learn Mandarin his pronunciation was erratic, which meant his meaning was sometimes unclear or mistaken. Erica's fluency helped him a lot.

Weeks passed and then months. One short loving letter arrived from Nikolei but had been censored and felt violated. After that she heard nothing more and the embassy knew nothing. Nothing!

Chapter 18

Lieutenant Baker called out to his driver to pull over but by the time the man had registered the order and manoeuvred out of the convoy, the jeep had travelled quite some distance and, although James jumped out even before it had stopped, he couldn't see Helena and the children back in the square.

Helena, for her part, momentarily thought perhaps she had mistaken that handsome face. How amazing that he should pass by after all this time and in a different part of the country. The boys were chattering to her now that the trucks had gone and so she pulled herself back from the sweet memories of her romance in Chongqing. Even as she thought of that, the guilt came flooding back, the feeling that maybe if she had been totally faithful to Fu Yan he wouldn't have been killed. She knew that was nonsense but it often nagged at the back of her mind.

Walking on towards the narrow market streets Helena heard her name called and turned to see James running through the crowd, head and shoulders above most of them. Unsure how to respond, she nevertheless realised that to walk on would be rude in such a public place, so she stopped and waited for him to reach them.

James stopped a few feet away from the little family group, taking in the difference in the young woman since they had met before. She had definitely lost some of her carefree glow, looked tense and tired even though still well dressed and confident. Catching his breath for a few moments he then said, "Helena, how good to see you. What are you doing here?"

"James, I could ask you the same. We live here."

In spite of all that they had shared, they were awkward with each other at first. For some minutes they exchanged formal pleasantries regarding how well they each looked (lies actually) and James admired the children. Then, almost in unison, they burst out laughing and the tension between them was broken.

"It's wonderful to see you Helena. I can't stop now but can we meet some time to catch up?"

"You mean you're staying here too?"

"Well not far away; there's a camp about ten miles down the road."

Throwing caution to the wind Helena replied, "Well we often come here or to the tea garden over there."

"I'll come as soon as I can, maybe tomorrow."

So saying, James waved and pushed his way back through the crowd to his waiting transport.

In the event, it was several days before James and Helena did meet again and she had begun to suspect that either he'd changed his mind or his regiment had been moved on.

When he did turn up, one chilly afternoon his first words were an apology for taking so long and he went on to explain that his duties had been changed by a new commanding officer at the camp.

"Never mind." smiled Helena. "You're here now."

"May I get you a cup of tea and something for the children?" asked James.

"Yes, that would be nice. Thank you."

Although Helena had hoped they would meet again, she had also been apprehensive as to how they would get along now their situation was so different. She need not have worried; from the very start they were comfortable with each other, as old friends. Occasionally the times in Chongqing were referred to but not in the sense of wanting to go back to the way they were.

Helena talked a lot that first day, explaining sadly all the things that had brought her to the situation she now found herself in.

James, too, had had an eventful time but had come through unscathed and was actually up for a promotion.

The time flew by and all too soon both had to hurry away, Helena to help with the evening meal and James back to the camp. They arranged to meet at the same time the following week and on the way home, as the boys chattered happily, Helena found her steps lighter than they had been for a long time. She had something to look forward to.

A few days later there was some more good news when Helena learnt that the little school the boys were attending was looking for some helpers. Being a foreigner she was not sure she would be accepted but in fact they were glad to have someone with knowledge of European languages because in recent months there had been further influxes of refugee children. The job wouldn't pay much but it would mean Helena could contribute something to the household expenses, be out of the house and have more to occupy her days.

Meeting up with James as arranged the following week, Helena looked and felt much more like her old self. She had taken more care with her hair, pressed her dress and put on a bright silk scarf, not to impress James but just because her spirits had lifted.

James was pleased to see that she looked a good deal better and was delighted to hear all about her new job which she had already started. Hearing that her aptitude for languages was helping her to move forward, he voiced the hope that their meetings and talking would be able to further improve her English.

"Oh, yes," said Helena, "I'm sure it will help a lot. Would you mind if I bring a notebook so I can begin to learn more words."

"Sure thing, Honey! No problem."

As it happened, some of the other staff at the school also had a smattering of English and so there was much sharing and mutual helping during break-times and lessons. Helena really began to feel she could count herself quite lucky with her new little job, four lovely children (although one was far away) and a roof over their heads.

Perhaps some time in the future they would be able to afford a place of their own and not feel a burden on Tao and Su Lin. From time to time Helena imagined changing up her gold "treasure" and moving out but something told her this would be the wrong time and the wrong place. She still had the little hoard of gold, collected over the years, well hidden at the bottom of her trunk and she had no intention of letting the cousins know about it. She had needed to use a little recently because she needed some suitable clothes for work and the children, the boys especially, were growing out of their winter clothes. Probably Su Lin had wondered how she had managed to acquire these things but she hadn't asked.

Helena's third bit of good news arrived shortly in the shape of a parcel of mail forwarded from Peking and containing a letter from her sister

Irmgard back in Germany, whom she hadn't heard from for a long time. The reason turned out to be that Irmgard, with her artistic talent, had managed to persuade their parents to let her study art and while doing so she had met a young man and was about to marry. The date on the letter showed it had been travelling for many months and no doubt they were already married. Thankfully Irmgard had had the fore-thought to give the address outside Berlin that they would move to.

As soon as the children were in bed Helena retired to the tiny cubicle that was her only private space to reply to her sister and also catch up on her correspondence to Erica and Gerda. She was glad to have so much positive news to write about and avoided the subject of the worsening atmosphere in the flat. This last came to a head a few weeks later when Helena found herself alone in the flat when Tao stumbled in the door and stood watching her. He had been drinking, which was unusual for most Chinese men and he looked very much the worse for it.

"Why are you avoiding me?" he leered.

"I don't know what you mean," replied Helena, keeping her eyes on the vegetables she was chopping.

"Don't give me that; I hear you are nice and friendly to soldiers!"

His tone was insinuating and insulting but Helena kept silent and gripped the knife tighter.

"It's obvious what type of woman you are, always being seen with Americans!"

"How dare you!" Helena rounded on him. "Lieutenant Baker is an officer and a gentleman and he's my friend."

Further unpleasantness was avoided by the sound of Su Lin's key in the door but Helena was shaking and she now knew for sure that she'd have to move out as soon as possible.

It proved even more difficult than Helena had feared to find a place to live, at any rate at a price she could afford. She didn't want to ask James for help at this point as he would probably want to subsidise her and she didn't want to be beholden to him in that way. Likewise if she started to raid her little cache of gold she felt she would find herself trapped.

All he colleagues at the little school knew she was trying to find somewhere and one day, some weeks later, a young woman mentioned that an apartment where she lived was coming vacant.

"It's not much mind, but it's affordable and I know you're keen to move, aren't you."

"I'm desperate to move. Where do you live?"

"If you like, we could go round after work."

So straight after school ended, the two young women made their way to the house. It was in one of the poorer areas of the city but reasonably close to the school and the market.

"The lady is called Madam Dzo, I'll get her and tell her you're interested."

After a few moments a door opened at the end of the dim corridor. Helena looked over and did a double-take for the diminutive Chinese woman, with her hair tightly drawn back and wearing a dark brocade gown, looked exactly like Fu Yan's mother

She regarded Helena with suspicion but nodded to her and beckoned her to follow her up two flights of rickety stairs.

The apartment consisted of two small rooms with one part sectioned off as a kitchen area. The only sanitation was back down those two flights of stairs. Although very basic and sparsely furnished, it was clean and the price was acceptable.

Helena held her breath after informing the old woman that she and her three young children would like to take the rooms. Thinking there was a hesitation, she quickly added "My children are young but they're very good and quiet at home."

Madam Dzo nodded and simply replied, "I like children."

It was clear that this was true; on the day they moved in the landlady's face changed immediately she caught sight of the little ones with their dark hair and oriental features. Her eyes softened, she smiled and patted each one of them. Before long she was visiting them in her spare time to play with the children and help them in writing their characters. Madam Dzo effectively became their surrogate grandma, often looking after them and bringing treats like salted plums and crisp-fried beans, much appreciated to supplement their meagre diet of rice porridge and pickled vegetables. What had seemed a desperate place to move to hadn't worked out bad at all.

Chapter 19

Sister Alice looked up from the exercise books she was marking and through the window saw Erica still sitting alone on the bench in the convent's small garden. The weather was really cold although the bitter Peking winter hadn't really began yet and the girl was bundled up in a thickly padded jacket but with nothing on her head. Her whole posture was of dejection and misery so different from the bright out-going young woman of a few months ago.

The young nun sighed and put away her books, drew a shawl around her and went out to sit with Erica and try to cheer her up but she knew there wasn't much she could do or say in the circumstances. Erica hardly looked up as her friend sat beside her but Alice could clearly see that she had been crying. Putting her arms around Erica, she handed her a clean white hankie and asked, "Still no news then?"

"It's worse than that! The embassy has posted him as missing in action and I've got to clear out of the apartment."

"Oh, my dear, I'm so sorry."

Every day for months Erica had been visiting the Russian Embassy to check for any news of Nick, ignoring the resigned looks on the faces of the Staff and the sometimes curt responses that she got. The routine gave structure to her days and almost stopped her thinking the unthinkable, though at night when she said her prayers a feeling of despair had taken hold of her. Today, finally, the elderly Ambassador had called her in and gently explained that they feared there was no more hope. The statistics of the dreadful losses at the front were withheld from her.

Sister Alice took her hand and though she knew the older sisters would use religious platitudes to comfort her, she simply said, "Remember you have lots of friends here – you are not alone."

Erica nodded and sighed deeply.

"Do you think I could stay at the convent? I don't really want to go back to our old house by myself. Anyway it's all shut up now."

"I think we can arrange that – I'll do my best. Come now into the kitchen. You need a hot cup of tea."

The warmth of the tea and the convent kitchen were cheering and the camomile content was calming.

"I'd better write to my mother in Xian to let her know but she can't really help me – she's struggling to keep herself and the little ones as it is."

Alice made no reply but gave her friend a quick hug and went off to finish her marking before evening prayers.

In due course Erica was installed into part of the convent that used to be kept for boarder students and she tried to immerse herself in her studies and helping the nuns with their teaching duties. Although she kept busy she was still clearly mourning her loss of Nick and the privileged life she had known. Her mood fluctuated between deep sadness and self-centred anger at the circumstances that had changed her life so dramatically. Sister Alice was becoming really worried about her friend because nothing seemed to lift her mood. The older nuns talked about the healing properties of Time and Prayer but Alice thought something more tangible was needed.

To this end she called on Father Martin to discuss a way forward.

Martin had heard about Erica's sad news and had offered condolences in the early days but as luck would have it he had been called away to a rural mission for some weeks and had only recently returned.

"Come in my dear, how nice to see you." He welcomed Sister Alice to his small house. "May I offer you some tea?"

"Thank you Father, but no, I have come to see you with a problem."

As Alice explained the situation and her concerns about Erica, Father Martin became increasingly troubled and sad that he had not realised what was happening to the girl.

"Of course it's natural that she should grieve," said Alice, "but it's been going on too long and she seems unable to get out of it. Have you any ideas?"

"I just think we must be positive and show her that her friends are all thinking of her."

Two days later Father Martin popped his head around the door of the classroom where Erica was helping some of the girls with their assignments.

"Could I have a quick word, Erica?"

"Of course, how can I help you?"

"It's my birthday tomorrow so I'm having a little soiree. My cook is making noodles for my longevity and pot-sticker dumplings; will you come?"

It was so long since Erica had had an invitation that her heart jumped and she smiled broadly.

"Oh, I love dumplings. Thank you, yes, I'll be there!"

"Wonderful, see you around six."

It's a birthday so she'd need to take a gift. No problem. Erica selected one of her earlier paintings for him.

It was a painting on a scroll, depicting two sinuous stylised fish among reeds. She thought he would like the simple forms and cool colours.

Now, what to wear, for so long she had been wearing plain dark colours as drab as the nuns but here was a chance to dress up. In her camphor wood chest she located her favourite jade green silk dress, made in the Cheongsam style. It clung to her figure, actually fitting a little better now that she had lost some weight.

Getting ready for the party was an almost forgotten pleasure and as she fixed her hair and applied some make-up she realised she was feeling as if she had come alive again. For one moment, as she pinned a pearl clasp that her father had given her into her hair, she wondered should she feel guilty about being happy. No – she shook herself and determined to enjoy the evening.

The party was a great success – the simple food delicious and the talk lively and friendly. One of the guests had brought along a birthday cake from the only remaining patisserie in Peking and thus the evening ended on a sweet note. Most of the guest were quite elderly and rose to leave soon after they had eaten the cake. Erica got up to leave as well but Martin placed a hand on her arm and said, "Please don't leave just yet. I have some rice wine I would like you to try."

The wine was pleasantly warming as they sipped from tiny porcelain cups in companionable silence, neither felt the need for conversation until Erica rose to leave, when Martin pressed another small drink on her and they fell to chatting about anything and everything.

At last Erica stood and said, "I must go it's almost curfew time."

Father Martin walked with her the few steps back to the convent and as they parted he took her hand and said, "I have enjoyed your company so much tonight. Thank you."

"Good night, Father."

In the weeks following they were often together. They walked by the lake and in the markets; they ate dim sum in tea houses and drank cocktails in the elegant hotels. Alice and the nuns were glad to see a return of the old lively and fun-loving Erica.

When they were together there was always lots to talk about: Erica shared the news that came from Xian in her mother's lively letters. She was very glad that Helena was now much more settled, enjoying her work and managing with the little ones. She also loved to hear her friend Martin talking about his boyhood and upbringing in Ireland.

As an Irish Catholic, of course, he came from a large family which had been poor but boisterous and happy, until his father was seriously injured in a farm accident. Then his mother began to clean other people's homes to make ends meet and her health inevitably suffered.

"They must be very proud that their eldest became a priest," said Erica.

"Oh, they were made up to be sure," laughed Martin, "though not so happy about me coming to China. The main thing is I'm still able to send money each month to help them out."

"Do you think you will return to Ireland when your work here is done?"

"The work in China will never be done but there are so many changes happening that no-one knows the future for China. We must trust God."

Before long, Father Martin was finding reasons to visit the convent, hoping to bump into Erica and making excuses to ask her to accompany him to the market or official meetings, grateful for her assistance with her superior knowledge of the Mandarin dialect. He did not question his own motives too carefully, convincing himself he was just doing his bit to cheer Erica up, as he and Sister Alice had agreed.

On the way back from many of their outings they would stop to enjoy a bowl of Hot and Sour Soup, a treat for the taste buds and a speciality of the region. One particular day, as they waited for their soup to be served, Martin was telling Erica about a letter he had received from one of his seminary colleagues who had been posted to Shanghai; surprised at how quiet she was, he looked closer and saw she was miles away.

"Are you alright, my dear? You're so quiet today."

"Yes, I'm sorry it's just that," her eyes filled with tears, "today would have been our wedding anniversary."

Seeing her crying had a profound effect on Martin. It was all he could do to keep from taking her in his arms but being in a public place he just handed her a hankie and patted her hand. The desire he felt at that moment meant he could no longer deny his feelings for her.

Back at home his thoughts and feelings were in turmoil—Erica filled his heart and soul but this could not be. He knew he should pray for guidance but somehow he couldn't, so he poured a glass of whisky and sat until the light had faded from the sky.

Unbeknown to Martin, Erica was also racked with guilt that she too should have felt desire for him in that way. This was a day she had been thinking of her dead husband and he is a priest—a man of God—what was she thinking of?

Independently they both arrived at the same conclusion: that the only thing to do was to avoid each other. It wasn't easy and sometimes the situation became difficult but then fate took a hand in the shape of a telegraph message from Xian.

BI-AN VERY SICK. MAY DIE. NEED HELP. PLEASE COME

Erica did not hesitate to make immediate arrangements to travel and pack up most of her things. Within a few days she was ready to leave, wondering when and if she would return to her beloved Peking.

Chapter 20

To obtain a seat on the weekly transport to Xian required some influence as did much in China in those days; this was forthcoming under the auspices of Madame Chiang after Erica enquired at the university admin office. For the daughter of the late Dean nothing was too much trouble.

The nuns had loaded Erica up with fruit and rice cakes so she had sustenance and at every stop there was someone to sell tea, so although it wasn't luxurious she was reasonably comfortable. On the bus itself most people chatted, some read, some slept.

In quiet times Erica found herself comparing this trip with the last time she had travelled to Xian. She and Nick had the luxury of private transport and they believed they had their whole lives ahead of them. Now she was beginning to understand the meaning of loss and realising the strength her mother had shown in carrying on for the sake of the children.

At last the rumbling vehicle drew into the noisy main square of Xian and disgorged its tired and dusty occupants. Erica immediately engaged a rickshaw and instructed the skinny coolie to take her mother's new address. She could see straightaway that they were heading to one of the poorer areas of the city and when he finally put down the yoke of his burden she gazed around with some dismay at the (in her opinion) seedy nature of the neighbourhood.

The area that their relatives had lived in hadn't been great but this was much worse. What on earth was her mother thinking about?

Gathering up her luggage and paying the man off, she headed into the depressing interior of the building calling out a general greeting to any occupant who may be in earshot. Madame Dzo poked her head out of her apartment looking very angry and icily asked, "Can I help you?"

"I'm looking for my mother Helena Yan, I believe she lives here with my brothers."

The old lady's face immediately softened and she broke into a toothless grin. "Oh you are Lana's girl, come, come I show you."

Helena had heard the exchange and was waiting at the door of their little apartment. Erica dropped her bags and ran to hug her mother and then the little ones huddled behind her. There were merry exchanges of joy at meeting again.

"Oh how you've grown," to the children. "How pretty you are." to her baby sister Chun.

The children were a little shy and nonplussed by the exuberant entry of their elder sister but soon settled and looked hopefully at Erica's luggage, wondering if there might be anything for them. Sure enough after a few minutes Erica delved about in her smallest bag and produced some sticky toffee apples that she had managed to buy from a trader at the last stop.

After a simple meal of vegetables and a few noodles in bone broth, the children were put to bed and the two women sat down together with a pot of tea to exchange news and generally catch up. Erica listened to her mother's account of poor little Bai An's illness. He had been suffering for weeks from awful stomach cramps which kept them all awake at night in spite of the herbal medicine that he was given. Helena had had to take several days off work as she hadn't felt able to leave him in spite of Madam Dzo's volunteering to care for him. This meant she hadn't got paid and making ends meet became even more difficult. She sighed and confessed to Erica, "Sometimes I felt at my wits end, I'm so glad you're here. It's so good to have someone to talk to."

Erica could hold back no longer. She burst out: "Why on earth are you living in this place, Mama? It's just awful!"

Helena sat back, feeling quite affronted.

"I had to find somewhere and this was all I could afford. I'm sorry if it doesn't suit you. Things have changed, you know, since your father died."

"Didn't Vati leave us well provided for then?" asked Erica, for the first time beginning to realise that her privileged life-style was in jeopardy.

"All I have is my wages and the savings that I've managed to make over the years. Your father's salary died with him and all the property was in Peking, now probably in the hands of the Japanese."

"Oh Mama, I didn't realise things were so tough. What are we going to do?"

They talked on long into the night about the loss of Nick and how the nuns and Father Martin had helped Erica. Mother and daughter cried a bit and did their best to comfort each other.

"At least now I'm here, I can help you look after the kids," said Erica as they prepared to go to bed, squashed together in Helena's hard bed.

Next morning Helena was up early preparing to go to work. As she rushed around the tiny apartment she called out a long list of instructions for Erica as to managing the children during the day. Although Bai

An was getting his strength back he was still not well enough to go back to school, so after taking Manfred to school Erica was to spend the rest of the day with the two little ones. At first she really enjoyed playing games with them, taking them out to walk around the city and discovering the liveliest parts of Xian for herself. After a few days, however, she began to feel her nanny's role very restrictive; she still enjoyed pushing them around the town, sometimes drawing admiring glances, for she and they made an attractive picture, but with very little cash in her bag she couldn't enjoy treating them or herself as she wished to.

Making her way back to the apartment as it was nearly time for Helena to return with Manfred, they heard the roar of several vehicles and turned to see three jeeps and a military transport truck approaching. Everyone around stood to watch and some, though not all, waved back to the Americans.

While in Peking Erica had sometimes seen American civilians and military personnel in the lively cosmopolitan venues and she knew they were good at enjoying themselves.

As soon as Helena got back Erica mentioned the troops she had seen and Bai An piped up, "We waved but we didn't see Jim-Jam?"

"Who's Jim-Jam?"

"Lieutenant James Baker – he's a friend from Chongqing."

"Oh, are they based nearby then?"

"Yes, the camp's just outside the town – not too far."

After supper they talked some more about 'the famous Jim-Jam,' Helena telling how they met up again quite by accident and how he had been instrumental really in her being able to get the job at the school. She did not mention how close they had been in Chongqing.

Erica's curiosity was aroused and she thought she might take a rickshaw ride out to the camp one day but before she could do so the circumstances of Bai An's illness overtook her. Three nights later he was so poorly again that Helena asked Erica to go down to Madam Dzo and ask her for some more of the medicine he had before. The older woman, whose nose had been put a bit out of joint by the arrival of Erica, made a bit of a fuss and muttered about the expense of the remedy but she did mix some up and gave it to Erica.

The little lad cried even more when he had to take the medicine and was promptly sick so it was doubtful how much actually got into his system. During the night he got worse and nobody got any sleep. Erica was very frightened and when her mother tried to give him some more medicine she grabbed it from her saying, "This vile stuff's no good. What is it anyway?"

"I think it's a ground-up root of some sort," sighed Helena.

"He needs some better medicine, Mama. I'm going to find some." So saying she grabbed her coat and ran out of the house.

At first she didn't really have a plan but as she left the alley she saw a rickshaw man resting on the corner and immediately an idea came to her. She would go to the military camp and seek help from the American lieutenant. The rickshaw coolie, really little more than a boy, looked a bit surprised when she called out her destination but he soon roused himself realising that the camp was quite a bit further than most of the trips around town so he could charge a bit more.

The ride out towards the camp was very bumpy and dusty and they encountered quite a lot of traffic because it was the time of day when peasants came into town from the outlying areas bringing small amounts of produce to sell or barter.

Once at the camp Erica jumped down, telling the boy to wait for her, and boldly approached the guard on duty. The young soldier was quite pleased to have the distraction of a lovely young woman – guard duty was generally very boring – but he had his orders and was no pushover. Consequently it took Erica quite a long time to convince him that Lieutenant Baker would want to speak to her, explaining the whole scenario of his friendship with Helena and the child's illness.

Eventually he told her to wait while he checked if the lieutenant was available and rang through to the main office. The reply seemed to take a very long time but at last he beckoned her over and said, "Miss, they're sending someone to escort you over, won't be long."

After what seemed an interminable wait but was probably only about ten minutes, a young Marine appeared marching smartly from the main prefabricated buildings. His march came to an abrupt halt very close to where she was standing and he turned to escort her back the way he had come but not before registering how attractive she was even while looking very worried. On the walk across the compound the young man shortened his steps to match Erica's and introduced himself as Franklin in order to find out her name. Although quite distracted by her mission, Erica smiled and gave her name

"Gee, that's really pretty, just like you," replied Franklin with a huge wink, that showed he really thought himself a great ladies' man.

At the office the Marine rapped smartly on the door and held it open for her to enter. Lieutenant Baker immediately rose from his desk and held out his hand.

"So you're Helena's grown-up daughter! I'm so pleased to meet you but the message I got said you and your Mama have a big problem?"

He gestured to a small wooden chair and after she sat down he returned behind his desk.

"I'm sure you wouldn't have come unless it was really important, so do tell me what the trouble is. Helena is not unwell is she?"

"No Lieutenant, it's my little brother Bai An. He's been so ill with stomach cramps and it's been going on for weeks. They give him this awful herbal medicine and I'm sure it's making him worse, so," Erica hesitated, "I thought maybe if you have some Western medicine…?"

"Mmm, I don't think we have much around the camp but I reckon it may be possible to pull in a few favours and get hold of something. It'll take a few days but I'll do my best, Honey."

"Oh, thank you, we'll be so grateful – I'm sure it's what he needs."

Lieutenant Baker rose and patted the girl's hand to reassure her.

"I'm sure you need to get back to your Mama. Give it a couple of days, then meet the supplies jeep in the main square at around noon. It'll be the Marine you just met, ok?"

Erica thanked him profusely and left feeling so much lighter in spirit. Franklin was standing smartly at attention outside the office ready to escort her off the camp. On the way back they chatted some more and Erica found she was looking forward to meeting him in a couple of days.

The rickshaw coolie was slumped by his vehicle practically asleep again but he soon roused and the ride back into town was clearer and quicker than the ride out.

Back at the house Erica ran up the stairs eager to tell her mother the good news that help would be coming soon but as soon as she opened the door she knew something was wrong. There was no sound of the children, the curtains were drawn and Helena was sitting in the dim little room with her head bowed.

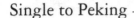

Fear clutched at Erica's stomach but unwilling to believe what the scene seemed to indicate she burst out, "Mama, I've seen James Baker and he's going to get some medicine for Bai An. It's going to be alright."

"No, Erica, thank you darling but it's too late."

Chapter 21

Madam Dzo proved to be a tower of strength yet again: she took charge of the arrangements for the burial and saw to it that the other children were fed and watered. At first Helena was apparently in a daze – hardly spoke, didn't weep – then quite soon she bustled about getting ready to back to work.

Returning from the market with a meagre basket of shopping that would provide their evening meal, Erica met the landlady on the stairs and was rather surprised to be asked in to take tea. The old lady reminded her, too, of her Chinese grandmother who had doted upon her and she soon found her quite pleasant company. Erica was glad of the chance to talk because she was worried about her mother's frame of mind.

"I can't understand, Madame Dzo. My mother doesn't seem to have taken in what has happened. She hasn't even cried for poor little Bai An." Erica's own eyes filled with tears which she tried to blink away.

"Sometimes, my dear, what life hands us is beyond tears. She will come to grieve in her own time. I think part of her almost expected it after his twin sister died. She told me he was never really robust. Don't worry, she'll be alright in time – she's a strong woman.

"I hope you're right." sighed Erica.

After finishing her tea and chatting some more, Erica rose to leave thanking her hostess for the tea and comfort and saying that she had shortly to go to the main square to tell the American that the medication they had hoped to procure was no longer needed.

In spite of herself and the sad nature of her mission Erica tidied her hair and put on a smart dress, wishing for a moment that she had bought with her the cream shoes and bag which matched this dress so much better. She made a mental note to add the request to send them when she wrote to Martin to tell him about the child's death. With a deep sigh, she promised herself to do that as soon as she returned from meeting the Marine; she always found letter-writing a bit of a chore, not like her mother who was such a good correspondent.

Marine Franklyn had arrived at the meeting place before Erica, deliberately on her part, and he relaxed with a cigarette while waiting for her and watching the buzz and bustle of the city. As she approached he let out a long low whistle and thought to himself what a stunning girl she was. Unfortunately she didn't look too pleased to see him but he understood why when, immediately on meeting, she explained that the medicine was no longer needed.

"Oh gee Honey, I'm real sorry to hear that and I'm sure the lieutenant will be too!"

"Thank you," replied Erica, blinking to keep back the tears. She hadn't expected to cry but the young man's kind sympathy had been the catalyst.

"What say we take a little walk and maybe find somewhere for a drink?" asked Franklyn, wondering if Eurasian girls were allowed or likely to accept invitations from Americans. To his delight Erica smiled and agreed.

Walking to the nearby tea garden was very pleasant and they talked easily together, keeping the conversation light as far as possible. All too soon it was time for Franklyn to get back to the camp, so they hurried back to the parked jeep where he handed Erica a small parcel containing the medicine and some sweets for the children.

"You might as well have the medicine anyway." He said "You never know. Say, in a couple of days I've got some free time, could we meet again?"

"I'd like that," replied Erica rather flirtatiously for she had enjoyed his company.

As soon as she got home she sat down to write the sad news to Father Martin and was still struggling with it when Helena arrived home from work.

Her mother's mood had changed from distracted to irritable and everything was wrong, from Erica using the table to the vegetables she had bought for their supper. Inevitably a row ensued with raised voices and the smaller children becoming upset; Little Chun was crying.

"I'm going out for a walk," muttered Erica sulkily.

"Fine, take them with you. I need a bit of peace!"

It was getting near to dusk and quite chilly so they didn't go far, just sat on a low wall sharing the sweets from Franklyn's parcel and watching some children playing a game in which they pretended to be martial arts champions.

The letter didn't get finished until the next day. Sealing the envelope and walking into town to post it, Erica's mind and heart were full of memories of her friendship with Father Martin. His companionship had always been so comforting; she'd felt safe with him and they had grown very close. If he hadn't been a priest it would have been so easy to fall in love with him. She didn't think he'd mind sending on the things she'd asked for, as long as he wasn't too busy, and she wondered if he would reply or just send a parcel.

In a surprisingly short time Martin did reply with a beautiful letter expressing his condolences and offering comfort to Erica and her mother in his eloquent style. He also said that he would ask Sister Ann to help to prepare the things that Erica had asked for. There was no news of his own life and although it was a kind letter, it was quite formal.

Each time Erica met Franklyn in the next few weeks he brought her some little gift of nylons or chocolate or chewing gum for the children. Once he even bought a pretty corsage of orchids and hibiscus. They had a good time together, laughing and chatting. He was good company and talked a lot about his ranch in America, obviously trying to impress her. There was little opportunity for them to be together in private and Erica actually thought this was probably a good thing for he was becoming more physical as time went on and although she found him attractive, it was never going to be a lasting relationship.

Walking arm in arm back to where the jeep was parked, Erica suddenly stopped with a gasp as she glimpsed Father Martin across the square surrounded by bags and parcels. At the same moment Martin saw her and their eyes met.

"What's up Honey? You ok?"

"I'm fine, it's just…That priest over there is a friend of mine."

Weaving their way through the traffic in the square, mostly donkey carts, porters and rickshaws, they reached the waiting priest and stopped a few feet away from him.

"Martin!" exclaimed Erica. "What are you doing here?"

"I came to bring your things, as you see."

"Oh, I didn't expect you to come personally."

"Obviously," replied Martin with an icy glance at the Marine.

"Oh Martin, this is Franklyn." The two men nodded at each other but did not shake hands.

"Glad to meet you," said Franklyn. "I'd like to help with the gear but I'm due back at camp right now." So saying, he crushed Erica to him, kissed her hard, on the lips and ran off to the parked jeep, calling, "See you soon, Honey."

Erica turned back to Martin with a smile which was immediately wiped away by the way he looked. His face was white and his lips a thin angry line.

"Erica, how could you go about with soldiers?"

"He's just a friend. We've been having fun together."

"So I see!"

Martin turned away from her shaking with jealous fury and without another word arranged for the luggage to go to the apartment. He followed the porters to see that nothing went astray.

At the doorway to the house Erica invited him to take some tea, greatly relieved to see that he seemed to have calmed down.

Helena and the children were at home and she greeted the priest cordially, glad to have some news of the way things were in Peking. Martin stayed for quite a while, chatting pleasantly and enjoying the company of the children and the two women.

At length he rose to go saying, "I'm must go and find my lodgings. Thank you for the tea."

"Do you have somewhere to stay?" asked Helena, hoping that he had because there was no way really that they could ask him to stay with them, especially with all the extra belongings Erica had sent for.

"Yes, I actually worked in Xian for a while a few years back, so I know the family at the mission and I have arranged to stay there for a time."

As they parted, Helena said she hoped they would see him again while he was in Xian. He and Erica exchanged glances and he said something non-committal.

"I'll walk a little way with you," said Erica and grabbed her jacket to follow him down the stairs.

At the bottom of the stairs Martin stopped. "Why do you think I came?" He asked.

"To bring my things I suppose," replied Erica.

"No!" said Martin, with a deep sigh. "I came because I had to see you. I can't live without you! I've tried but it's impossible."

Unable to make a reply, Erica just gazed at him and in that moment they both knew she loved him too.

Martin gently took her hand and bent to kiss it. Instinctively Erica reached out to him and in a moment she was in his arms lost in a deeply passionate kiss.

When they pulled apart, Martin turned without another word and walked away, not even looking back. His senses were reeling, his heart filled with a mixture of joy and fear.

Back in the flat Helena had finished tidying as much as she could.

"What a nice man he is. So kind of him to bring your things but I don't know how we're going to find space for them all."

"Don't worry about it Mama, I was thinking I'll probably sell some of it and that will help out with the housekeeping."

"Mmm, that's quite a good idea. You won't need lots of these things here," she said, holding up a peach-coloured gossamer-light ball gown.

It was a gown that Nikolei had loved and in that moment Erica rather wished she hadn't kept it.

"Still, it was really nice of Father Martin to bring it all over. We should do something to thank him. Do you think we'll see him again before he goes back?"

"Oh yes, I think so. In fact, I'm sure."

Chapter 22

Martin was greeted at the mission House like a long-lost friend and made to feel really welcome immediately. The pastor's wife had made soda bread and vegetable soup, knowing his Irish background, a wonderful way to make him feel at home and comfortable.

As the meal had been ready for some time they sat down to eat almost straight away and were joined by two other priests who were also staying at the house. The simple but wholesome fare and the friendly atmosphere over the meal soon meant that the conversation progressed from small talk of new acquaintances to really thoughtful discussions and the sharing of life experiences.

Inevitably the politics of China and her current situation were almost the keystone of all the talk that evening. Martin had wondered that neither of the priests was wearing the cloth of their order, even though they had been introduced by their clerical names but it was soon explained that both of them had fled from nearby provinces due to the advance of Communist troops. Both Fathers had disturbing tales to tell of colleagues who had 'disappeared', of church property that had been confiscated, destroyed or ransacked.

At present Xian was safe enough but both men felt safer by keeping a low profile. Their future was uncertain but it seemed likely that both would leave China at any rate for a time, perhaps to go to Hong Kong.

The younger of the two priests became very emotional when he talked about his guilt at abandoning the work he had been called to and loved. The others comforted him as best they could and all prepared to retire for the night.

Martin climbed wearily into the hard narrow bunk he had been allocated and pulled up the thin woollen blanket. For quite a while he couldn't sleep; not because of the physical discomfort but because his mind was full of things he'd heard tonight and the feelings he knew he had for Erica. Eventually he fell asleep knowing that he had an awful lot of thinking to do in the next few days.

After breakfast, consisting of a small bowl of the inevitable rice porridge, Martin and the other guests set about helping with chores which was the only cost of staying at the mission. Once the chores were done the group held a short prayer meeting and Martin found the familiar words and sense of ritual helped to calm the conflicting thoughts in his mind. It didn't last long and then the group separated to go about their own business for the day.

Martin donned his hat and jacket and left the mission, walking out into a cool but bright morning. At first his steps led him towards the apartment he had left last evening but after a short distance he stopped and took a different direction. His walk then took him towards the old city wall where he walked along the ramparts passing the distinctive Bell Tower. The area was quiet and serene with the beautiful Mount Li in the background but Martin was totally unaware of the scenery or his surroundings. He walked and walked, deep in thought.

He must decide what was right. He must work out what to do for the best. Turning last night's conversation over in his mind, Martin began to feel conscious of his clerical garb and a little uncomfortable in it for the very first time since he had been ordained, even though there were very few passersby and those there were, largely ignored him. The thought came to him that if he too abandoned the soutane he would feel he was denying his identity.

It was almost dark when Martin began to make his way back to the mission, not really any further forward in his dilemma. He loved a woman and he loved the Church – what could he do? The only decision he had come to was to write to his bishop in Peking, a man who had always been a good friend.

It was three days since Erica had seen Martin. She had expected him to return the next day after the way he had kissed and held her. She didn't know exactly where he was staying but it couldn't be that far away.

Her emotions fluctuated time after time between concern that something could be wrong and annoyance that she had no word from him. She stayed in most of the time, expecting him to call and had avoided the places she thought she might meet Franklyn. Well, perhaps she'd waited long enough.

Almost as soon as that thought occurred to her there was a knock at the door and when she opened it, there was Martin, smiling his gentle thoughtful smile.

"I thought you'd forgotten where I live," she said sulkily, although her heart was singing at the sight of him. He really was a handsome man, dressed today in dark coloured Western style dress, not his familiar cassock.

Martin ignored her petulance, just stepped close to her and took her hand, placing a soft kiss in her palm. Erica melted inside and smiled as he whispered

"Shall we go for a walk?"

She grabbed her coat and shoes and they left the house together, without speaking. It was enough to be together, walking in the soft sunlight, both barely aware of their surroundings.

They took the same route that Martin had been continually walking over the past few days. Erica was enchanted by the architecture and the peaceful atmosphere on the city wall. They passed the Bell Tower and the Drum Tower and Martin explained that they were both symbols of the city of Xian. Erica wondered if she might someday incorporate one or both structures into one of her paintings and she determined to either take some photos or at least do a sketch as soon as she could.

After a time, as they walked, Martin took her hand, both feeling shy but wonderfully close in this simple gesture. It occurred to Erica that Martin only felt able to show affection to her in public because he was not in 'uniform' of his Holy Order but she didn't really feel able to voice this thought. His intuition though voiced it for her and he began to explain about the other priests he had met at the mission. Without making a big deal of it he talked about potential danger to himself and to his associates from hard-line Communist groups.

"Although it seems that Xian is still safe I wouldn't want to be the cause of bringing any trouble to you or your family."

Erica nodded, understanding and appreciating his concerns.

They slowly made their way back to the apartment as Erica had to collect the children and begin to prepare supper. Before they parted

Erica remembered that Helena had suggested inviting him as a 'Thank you' and so she asked him to supper the following day, trusting that her mother would agree.

Helena readily agreed that Martin should visit for supper and gave Erica a little extra cash to use for the meal. Although Erica wasn't much of a cook, she had helped out in the convent kitchen sometimes and was able to call on that experience. She bought some tofu to add to their usual vegetable dishes and put in plenty of ginger root to give a spicy tang.

When Martin arrived he had brought some sesame sweets for the children and a small bottle of rice wine. As they sat to eat he prepared to say a Grace but before he did Helena asked if he would first say a little prayer for 'for poor little Bai An'.

"Of course, my dear," he replied and after a few moments though, he gave a beautiful thoughtful eulogy in his soft Irish voice. The gentle words brought tears to all of their eyes. Seeing tears in her mother's eyes Erica realised that at last she was starting to enter the phase of grieving for her lost boy.

Supper was a great success, the food surprisingly tasty for once and even the children ate well. When the meal was over Helena put the little ones to bed while Martin helped Erica to clear away and wash up. The three of them then sat down together and the rice wine was poured into tiny cups. Each made a different toast

"Prosit," from Helena.

"Gambei," from Erica

"Slainte," from Martin.

At the first taste they all winced a bit for the wine was a strong herbal type of spirit that the elderly Chinese often used as a tonic.

"Whew. My old granddad in Ireland used to make poteen in his shed and I thought that tasted bad, but this is worse!"

They all laughed and this comment led to some more stories about life back in Ireland. As the evening progressed the conversation ranged widely as they talked about the current situation in Peking and China in general. Martin was strongly of the opinion that China was becoming increasingly dangerous for foreigners of any persuasion.

Helena really enjoyed reminiscing with Martin about her life in Peking which seemed light years away from what she had now. Perhaps the rice wine loosened her tongue a little but she told him all about the early antipathy from Fu Yan's mother and how grateful she was and still is for the friendship of Gerda.

"Oh, are you still in contact with this lady then?" asked Martin.

"We write regularly. She is in Formosa with her Chinese husband and family. They have a beautiful home there –she sent some pictures." Helena sighed and continued, "Every letter she asks me to come and bring the children and actually the last letter was really begging me to think about our safety because of the political situation in China. Gerda's husband is in diplomatic service and very influential. She's invited us to stay with them until I get settled – I must admit I'm beginning to think it might be best."

Martin nodded and sipped a little more wine, finishing the drink before rising to leave.

"Thank you so much for your hospitality. I have enjoyed your company so much. I hope we'll meet again before I return to Peking."

"I'll see you out," cried Erica, Jumping up to go with him to the door.

After he had left, Helena looked thoughtfully at her daughter.

"He's given us a lot to think about. A very nice man but be careful, you don't get too fond of him. He's a priest so there is no future in it."

"I know, he's just a friend," replied Erica as she cleared the cups and wine and got ready for bed.

Chapter 23

Just a few days later Martin called to say goodbye, as he had obtained a transfer back to Peking much earlier than anticipated.

Always forthright and seeing that he was still wearing lay Western clothes Helena asked, "Have you totally given up wearing your soutane now, then?"

"I have it in my bag but I think it's better to wear ordinary clothes until I see how the land lies. I hope you don't think that's cowardly."

"No, no –I just wondered, but what if someone wants to see your papers?"

"Well I think it's safer if I say I'm a journalist."

"Oh, yes," piped up Erica. "You would make a marvellous journalist – you are so good with words and ideas. I'm sure you would do well."

Martin smiled sheepishly and said "Yes, if it comes to that, I think I could make a living that way."

As he left they promised to keep in touch and Martin's last words were "God be with you all."

As they shut the door Helena muttered, "Huh, he seems to use God only when it's convenient."

Erica didn't reply – she was busy with her own thoughts.

Feeling at a bit of a loose end since Martin had left and as she no longer saw Franklyn, Erica remembered her plan to revisit the Bell Tower and the Drum Tower so she searched among the things that Martin had brought for her small camera which she thought she had seen there. She found it after a while inside another bag and was glad to see it still had film. Her mother was at work and the children didn't need to be collected for hours yet so she set off to walk along the city wall and indulge her artistic talent. With the camera swinging from her shoulder she made her way past a group of rickshaw coolies and towards the crowded market place. She didn't get as far as the Towers – it was as though simply having the camera on her person made her look with new eyes at the everyday scenes in the town.

Before she knew it she'd completed the film with shots of the Chinese people in their environment, some partly posed but many candid showing the poor but proud population going about their daily lives. As the reel of film came to an end Erica realised that she had rarely enjoyed an afternoon so much and that it was time to hurry to collect her brother and sister.

After the children were in bed the two women drank some tea and Erica told her mother how much she'd enjoyed her afternoon behind the camera lens.

"Now I have to find someone to develop and print the pictures of course. You don't know of anyone, do you Mama?"

"No, it's not something I've ever thought of here. If we were back in Peking I could tell you one or two places – Vati was quite keen on taking photos – took lots of you when you were little." She sighed and was silent for a few minutes before continuing. "Probably the best person to ask would be Madam Dzo – she knows just about everything that goes on in this city."

Erica nodded and agreed "Yes, Mama, I got that feeling too."

First thing next morning Erica duly picked up her camera and knocked politely on Madam Dzo's door. She was welcomed in and pressed to take some tea from the ever-warm pot. The old lady reminded Erica even more of her grandmother as she sat back in her chair, resting her hands over her stomach and nodding at the camera said, "You'll need to go to old Machu; his little shop is in the third alley behind the market – if you can't find it, just ask anyone."

"How did you know I wanted to ask about the printing?" asked Erica.

"It's obvious, camera's no good otherwise. But I'm a bit disappointed that you haven't taken a picture of me yet."

"Oh, I'm sorry I've run out of film but I promise I'll take a lovely one as soon as I get more film. Do you think this Machu will have film as well?"

Madam Dzo shrugged and replied, "I daresay. Now before you go tell me all about that young man who came the other night."

It was easy to find old Machu's business but as Erica approached it she didn't feel awfully confident. She pushed open the ramshackle door and entered what resembled a scruffy and very down-market pawn brokers. In the middle of the room the old man was seated cross-legged, tapping away on a large abacus. He didn't look up so Erica judged it might be a good idea to mention Madam Dzo.

She cleared her throat and said, "Zao'an (Good Morning). Madam Dzo said you might be able to develop this film for me?"

The old fellow looked up and grinned a gappy grin without pausing for a moment in his calculations. He stretched out a hand for the film and popped it into the sleeve of his robe. Taking this as agreeing to the job Erica ventured to ask, "Do you have any more film as well?"

"Maybe, maybe," he muttered, pottering of into a dark back room and returning quite quickly with two new rolls.

"Oh, that's terrific," smiled Erica. "How much?"

Amazingly he just went back to the abacus and replied, "Pay me when you come for the pictures. Come day after tomorrow."

"Oh, thank you. Good bye."

She found she couldn't wait to get back and load the film so she could take more photos. Today she planned to visit some of the nearby temples and shrines to record something of the religious life of the people.

Back at home later Erica didn't mention the encounter or her day's occupation to her mother, thinking she would wait and see how the pictures came out first.

On returning to collect the photos on the appointed day, Erica on first sight of them was delighted with the results. She then carefully placed them on the counter to observe them still further before she left the shop because Madam Dzo had warned her that Machu could be unscrupulous when it came to business. He smiled to himself as she inspected each one and pleased her by nodding encouragingly and saying, "They are good pictures. Are you going to sell them?"

"Oh, I hadn't really thought," replied Erica. "Do you really think they're good enough?"

"Well," said the wily old chap, "They're quite good but you could do better with a better camera." So saying he pottered off into the back room and returned carrying a high quality German camera.

"I could let you have this one for a good price."

Erica took it from him to check it and get the feeling of it. From the first moment she coveted it.

"Would you take my camera in part-exchange?" she asked.

"Oh, yes, this is normal, but that's a much more valuable camera."

"Mmm. I would like to have it. I'll need to ask my mother. Keep it for me until tomorrow."

On the way home Erica was walking on air – buoyed up with her project and the praise she'd received. If she could persuade Helena to let her have a better camera, she felt sure she could prepare a superb portfolio of pictures and then – maybe she could become a professional photographer, even a photojournalist. If she got work on a well known magazine she could even become famous AND she could find a decent place to live! By the time she got home she had convinced herself that this was where her future lay.

At home she arranged the pictures artistically to show them to their best advantage and waited for her mother to return. Madame Dzo came in first with the children and she too exclaimed over them appreciatively. The children were mildly interested and had to be threatened to keep their sticky fingers off them.

Helena's reaction wasn't so pleasing; although she said they were good she was not best pleased that they were all over the table preventing them from laying up for supper.

"You haven't even looked at them properly," wailed Erica as she hurriedly gathered her precious pictures together and cleared them out of the way.

"I'll look at them again later, ok!"

Disgruntled, Erica put the photos away safely and decided to bide her time because she knew if she was going to persuade her mother to part with some money for the new camera, she would have to choose the right time.

After the children had gone to bed the pictures were brought out again and this time Helena's attitude was quite different, especially when Erica explained about her idea of producing a portfolio with a view to taking up photography professionally. Of course the sting in the tail was that she needed money for the better camera but even this didn't detract from the fact that here was the first time her daughter had ever considered earning her own living. Up until then she had always expected everything she required to fall into her lap, which of course it generally had.

After thinking for a few minutes as she continued to gaze at the images before her, Helena got up and went to her top drawer. She held out her hand to Erica saying, "I haven't got much cash to let you have but you could take these earrings. They're solid gold, so they surely will be enough."

"Oh, thank you, Mama," cried Erica, jumping up to hug her mother and spin her around.

Next day the negotiations for the camera were successfully completed and over the next few weeks Erica was almost never separated from her prized possession. She worked thoughtfully, producing a superb pictorial portfolio: wide ranging and technically accurate it contained every genre from artistic portraits to romantic landscapes. She was encouraged every step of the way by old Machu and felt really delighted that her plans were taking shape.

Unknown to Erica, Helena was also making plans and had started to make tentative enquires about getting them all to safety in Formosa.

The plans of the two women collided one evening when a knock on the door revealed a message from James Baker asking Helena to see him next morning with regard to a passage to Free China.

"Oh, you've decided to go to Formosa, have you?"

"Yes, another move. We seem to have become gypsies don't we? I just hope James can arrange something soon, then I can write to Gerda to let her know we're coming." Helena paused and then continued, "I just hope it won't take too long to get settled – I don't want to impose on Gerda for too long – she's really good but taking in four people is a lot to ask."

"Four people? I'm not coming!"

"What? What do you mean? You can't stay here."

"No," replied Erica. I'm going to Shanghai. Martin's there already working as a freelance journalist and he can probably get me some work in photography."

Helena could hardly believe her ears and was speechless for a few minutes while Erica continued to expand her plans and dreams about how busy and lively Shanghai would be and how she was looking forward to it.

"Well," said Helena finally, "I can't stop you but I think you're crazy and how exactly do you intend to pay for your fare?"

"I guess I'll have to sell something or maybe I could ask Martin to send me the money."

"You'll do no such thing – we'll work something out. You've given me a real shock – I'm going to bed.

Helena waited until Erica was fast asleep before going to her wardrobe to the precious stash of gold. She removed two small ingots from the bag and carefully replaced it in its hiding place. She wasn't going to let anyone discover that hiding place – even her daughter. The

gold bars that she had so carefully hoarded over these years represented her security and her future.

Chapter 24

Sleep still didn't come to Helena for a very long time. The 'bombshell' that her daughter had just dropped on her and its implications kept going round in her head. It hadn't occurred to her until now that Erica's eagerness to call into the mailbox office to collect any letters was anything more than desire to help; she then had to wonder what else had she kept secret.

As she tossed and turned, Helena remembered that other huge shock when she had learnt that Erica had kept her marriage to the Russian a secret. In the light of that, this wasn't really surprising, but what a worry that the girl (woman) was so headstrong. What might she do next? At last Helena drifted off, having resolved to insist upon knowing more details of Erica's plans before making any mention of the gold for her fare.

In the morning, straight after their simple breakfast of steamed buns, the children were sent to play in the small backyard where Madame Dzo was always happy to keep an eye on them. Helena then turned to face Erica with her hands on her hips, looking quite fearsome.

Erica gulped and opened her mouth to speak, but her mother spoke first: "No, you listen to me! I am very disappointed that you were so deceitful in keeping your letters secret. It seems to me you always want your own way and never mind anyone else."

Erica tried to interrupt again but Helena was on a roll, "Look how crafty you were in making sure you stayed in Peking when you should really have come with us to Chonqing. Then you went and got married without telling anyone, now this! Planning to go to the other side of China where you know no-one!"

"It's no worse than you travelling from Germany to China where you only knew one person too!" retorted Erica. Helena had no answer to that so Erica went on "I wasn't really being deceitful, I just didn't want to say anything until it was all settled. Here's the letter, you can read it for yourself."

Dearest Erica

I'm writing sooner than I thought because the situation has changed so much in Peking. I know you didn't really want to go to Formosa with your family and had thought of returning to Peking – don't do so – it isn't safe here! As soon as I arrived I went to the bishop's house, he was my friend and mentor – but the housekeeper was so obstructive I had to virtually force my way in. When I did, she said, "It's no good he's not here – he's gone." As you know my Mandarin is not perfect but eventually I understood that she meant he had gone for good. She didn't seem to know where he had gone but as I left I saw that she seemed to have filled the house with lodgers or family – I don't know which. At my little house it was almost worse; I opened the door – never locked as you know, and called out to Fu Lo. There was

no reply and the rooms had such a strange feeling as though
everything had been abandoned. I felt as though I were aboard
the 'Marie Celeste'. I stayed that night, needing somewhere to
sleep and luckily met my old neighbour; a gentle man of the
Buddhist persuasion, who advised me that all religions were
being persecuted and much property being claimed. He knew I
was a priest, obviously, and sadly he congratulated me on my
'disguise'. I know I have to pack up and go soon and, in the not
too distant future, probably leave China altogether though it
will break my heart. Shanghai seems to be the best place to go
– there's still a large foreign population there and of course it's
an international port with connections all over the world. I will
write to you when I reach my destination but please heed what
I say and, whatever you decide to do, don't go back to Peking.
My thoughts are with you and your family
Martin

Helena handed the letter back and sighed, "What a world we live in! But he's not even in Shanghai according to that."

"No, but I got another short note saying he had found digs in Shanghai and he's got a job – it must be easy to get work there."

"It's not easy to get work anywhere and even harder to keep it, as you'll find out." replied her mother.

Erica's whole body language was confident determination and Helena was just too tired to argue any more.

Both women in the next few weeks were pre-occupied with making plans for their future but they made sure each evening to spend some time together chatting about good times and making sure the bond between them stayed strong. It was in many ways an anxious time as well as an exciting one.

In Shanghai Martin was dipping his toe into the secular life of that vibrant city and rather enjoying it. His half-formed plan to try journalism had led him to rough out a couple of articles about life in Peking 'before and after' as it were and this project occupied him during the journey from Peking where there were several changes and long delays.

On arrival in the city he had headed away from the prosperous commercial centre to quieter streets in search of digs that would be more affordable. It wasn't too difficult – he soon found an elderly Chinese couple who would be glad of the money in exchange for a small but clean room and one meal a day. As soon as he had rested up he set to work on tidying up the articles he'd written, ready to submit them to one or two journals. Believing that there was nothing like a personal approach, he tucked his briefcase under his arm and set out to find his way to the newspaper offices.

The centre of Shanghai was unlike any city he'd ever been in before: the smart and innovative buildings everywhere seemed more like he had imagined America than any part of China. Telling himself he had no time to spend sightseeing, he sought a likely spot to get some information about newspaper or magazine offices. He chose a large hotel and marched confidently up to the reception desk. The middle-aged Chinese man behind the desk gave a new dimension to the word 'inscrutable' and seemed determined not to understand and certainly not to give anything away.

Ah, well. You can't win them all, thought Martin as he politely thanked the chap for nothing and began to walk away.

"Excuse me! Perhaps I can help?" A clear and very cultured voice rang out from one of the deep leather chairs in the lounge area. Martin turned and met the gaze of a smoothly-dressed white-haired man, smoking a large cigar.

"I am just about to visit one of the large newspapers nearby, perhaps you would like to walk with me?"

"Oh, that's most kind of you, Sir. Thank you."

As the older man rose, Martin extended his hand and introduced himself. There was a firm handshake but no reciprocating introduction.

Together, they left the hotel without a backward glance and strolled along the street. During the short walk Martin explained his purpose and tapped the briefcase containing the sample article. He also explained a bit about the background to the article, more than anything to fill the silence between him and his acquaintance.

The office they were heading for was on the third floor of a large and imposing building and they rode in a small and very slow lift to reach it.

"That's the fellow you need to see – over there." The older man waved his arm towards a large desk in the corner and breezed on through the room to a glass- fronted office.

"Thank you so much, Sir. Thank you for your help."

"No problem. No problem," and he was gone.

Martin took a deep breath, cleared his throat and approached the desk. The occupant of the desk was looking harassed but he immediately motioned Martin to take a seat opposite him.

With a broad grin and an even broader American accent Phil, the copy editor, introduced himself and said, "Well, walking in with the boss is sure the best way to get seen! What can I do for you?"

"That gentleman is your boss?"

"In that he pretty well owns the paper, yeah."

Lady Luck or someone is certainly on my side today, thought Martin as he opened his briefcase and explained a bit of background to the article.

He handed the sheets over, fully expecting to see them shoved into a drawer but Phil took them, gave him a shrewd and piercing look and proceeded to skim read the article.

Looking up, he nodded approvingly. "It's good. We might need to tweak it a bit but I think we can use it."

"Really that's great," replied Martin and then hesitated, unsure how to approach the question of payment.

Phil came to his rescue by asking, "Do you see this as a one-off or have you more ideas?"

"Oh, I'm thinking I don't have a future in the Church in China any more so I need to come up with another way of life really."

"I'm not surprised actually," said Phil, "we've had a lot of missionaries both ordained and lay people come through the city – most feel they're leaving China for good."

Both men sat silent for a moment. Then Phil brightened and said, "Come on let's discuss this over a couple of whisky sours." In jubilant mood they made their way back to the hotel that Martin had left less than an hour ago and he couldn't resist a smug glance at the unhelpful receptionist.

As sometimes happens, the two men found themselves forging a firm friendship quite rapidly: although from very different backgrounds they found they held very similar views, attitudes and principles. The two whisky sours soon became two more and by the time Martin made his way, a little unsteadily, back to his digs he felt much more optimistic about the future.

The payment for a published article by a freelance writer was much more than Martin had expected and his first thought was to leave his frugal lodgings and move somewhere more up-market but then he remembered how important his rent was to the old couple so he decided to stay put. In any case, he thought, it would be necessary to save some money for the time that he might need to move on.

Packing wasn't easy at all. What to take? What to leave? And although Erica was excited about the prospect of the trip and a fresh start in Shanghai, she was still sad to be leaving her little brother and sister, especially when Manfred asked "Can I come with you?"

"No, Sweetheart. I'm sorry, not this time, but maybe when you're a bit older, ok?"

The arrangements for the travel were made using one of the two gold bars that her mother had given her. She paid only the first part of her journey to begin with because she would be travelling by rail from Xian to Wuchang where it would be necessary to catch a steamer down the Yangtze to Shanghai.

The evening before she was due to leave Erica bought some finely minced pork so they could make pot-sticker dumplings for a treat. Erica prepared the filling, Helena made the dough and even the children could help by breaking portions of dough off the long sausage of dough and rolling them thinly into rounds. When they were almost ready to cook, Helena said, "Manfred, go and ask Madam Dzo if she would like to come and share our meal. Tell her we're having dumplings."

Madam Dzo was expecting him as Erica had already invited her earlier and she had made a little bowl of dipping sauce with vinegar, chilli and best quality soy.

Everyone enjoyed the dumplings and they had a lovely evening. When Madam Dzo rose to leave she hugged Erica and fervently wished her good luck and blessings, for she had grown fond of all of the family in the short time she had known them.

In the morning Manfred ran to the corner to call two rickshaw coolies to take them and all the luggage to the station. The platform was in utter chaos: mountains of luggage, hundreds of people and even some livestock. They managed to find Erica's carriage and squeezed her and her luggage into the compartment but it wasn't going to be a comfortable journey. Helena checked again that she had Gerda's address safely and made Erica promise to write regularly.

"I wish I had an address for you," she said, "so send me one as soon as you know where you are staying."

"I will. But in any case Martin has a job with the Shanghai Evening Post so you can contact us there if you need to," replied Erica.

Just then the whistle sounded and the engine emitted a huge hiss of steam. There were few remaining on the platform to wave the travellers off, mostly just elderly people who all waved until the train was out of sight.

There were a great many stops on the train journey, some scheduled, some not. The passengers, mostly Chinese, were placid and accepting of the delays although there was little information as to the reasons. At the scheduled stops it was usually possible to disembark and purchase snacks or various street-food offerings, some of which Erica found delicious. When the track ran near highways they often passed large groups of people, apparently refugees, trudging along carrying whatever they could. At some points it seemed as if the whole of China was on the move.

At last, signalled by a general hubbub in the carriage, the journey was nearly over and the great Yangtze River came into view.

She had been told it would be easy to get a boat down to Shanghai –
it wasn't anything of the sort. For a start, when everyone piled off the
train there were very few coolies to help with the luggage so she ended
up struggling like anything and in the end dumping one case in a corner,
intending to come back for it when she had found a boat. There was
no booking office; it appeared you had to either approach the vessels
personally or risk trusting one of the dodgy-looking 'agents' who were
hanging about near the dockside. In the end this was what she did and
after a very long wait he returned and demanded an extortionate price
for passage on a filthy-looking cargo steamer.

Erica didn't know what to do for the best, but she couldn't go back so
she haggled with the man and got the price down a bit. He grudgingly
accepted and at least did help her on with her luggage.

If the train had been uncomfortable, this was purgatory: There were
clearly too many passengers on the ship and they were crammed into
one 'Rest Area'. Looking back later, Erica couldn't think how she
survived those awful few days with virtually no rest, no privacy and
the most basic ghastly food.

When the tall buildings of Shanghai came into view she almost wept
with relief as did many of the others on board.

Thank goodness there were plenty of porters around on the dockside
to help with the luggage and Erica even managed to get a modern taxi
into the city.

"Where to, Miss?" asked the driver.

"A good hotel, please," replied Erica, sinking back into the seat with
a deep sigh.

"I'll take you to the very best place – really good hotel, no problem!"

grinned the driver as he pulled out into the traffic and bullied his way through pedestrians and rickshaws.

Mmm, thought Erica, that probably means really expensive but she was past caring, just desperate for a hot bath and some sleep.

After checking into the hotel, more porters took her luggage to the room and, as the door closed behind her, she took in the calm elegance and knew she had made the right decision. The soup noodles she had ordered from reception arrived promptly and after savouring that she found she couldn't keep her eyes open. The bath would have to wait.

A short nap refreshed her and she was soon luxuriating in deep hot water. She washed her hair and pinned it so it would dry in waves. Beginning the unpacking, she managed to locate a pretty midnight blue dress, which she knew clung in all the right places, and the shoes which matched it. A little silver bag completed the outfit and when she crossed the lobby to the dining room for dinner, every head turned.

"Well, you're a dark horse, Martin," called Phil as the paper's newest freelance writer called in to check for possible assignments.

"What do you mean?" answered Martin.

"Just that there's been a beautiful young woman asking after you."

Immediately Martin knew it must be Erica and his heart did a little flip. Trying to appear nonchalant, he said, "Oh, did she leave a name?"

"No, but she left you a note," grinned Phil, handing him an envelope.

"Thanks, I'll read it later," said Martin, popping it in his pocket.

There was no work for him at the office today so Martin left soon after. Phil watched him go thoughtfully – was the guy really a priest or not?

As soon as Martin read the note he went round to the hotel. Walking into the foyer, he looked around and saw a group of ladies chatting in the lounge area. Erica was among them. They were mostly wives from the nearby consulate area who liked to meet in the hotel for tea or cocktails and who had kindly invited Erica to join them, seeing that she was alone. He stood for a moment, unsure whether to intrude, but almost immediately Erica looked across and their eyes met!

Chapter 25

With Erica gone, the flat seemed quite empty; Helena had thought she would be glad of the extra space and up to a point she was, but she did miss her daughter's lively companionship and the children really missed the fun they had with her. Now she knew she really had to take the bull by the horns and make a move to Formosa for the sake of the children's future. Up until now she had persisted, in a half-hearted way, in teaching Manfred and Chun some German against the time they would be able to return to her homeland but she had now accepted that it wouldn't be possible, at least in the foreseeable future. Although she hadn't heard from James for quite a while, she knew he wouldn't forget her and his promise to help.

James had been touchingly concerned when Helena had made the enquiries about travel to Free China, wondering where she would stay and how they would manage. He had been glad to hear she would be staying for a time with Gerda as he, of course, remembered Gerda from way back in Chongqing when they met. Even though she trusted him implicitly, Helena had not mentioned the gold she still had and which she intended to carry wrapped around her body as before. She was grateful when he explained that as it would be on military aircraft no cost would be incurred; it would be under the heading of evacuation.

Helena had not spoken to the children about leaving, not wanting to unsettle them yet again but she kept waking in the night, worrying and wondering how she would manage all the packing.

On the way home from work one afternoon, rushing as always to buy something for supper from a market stall, Helena heard a couple of short sharp hoots and turned to see James heading towards her in an open jeep.

She waved and stopped while he pulled up across the way and jumped out. She scanned his face, wondering if he had good news, but was unable to tell anything from his expression.

As he came up to her he stopped and formally shook her hand. "Good afternoon Helena. I was hoping I'd run into you. I have some news for you."

Helena gasped. Although she had been hoping for news of a flight, if it was imminent she felt quite anxious.

"Have you got us a flight to Formosa?" she cried, gripping on to his arm.

"Hold on, hold on. It's not a hundred per cent just yet but I think the arrangements will soon be finalised."

"When do we go? Oh, I have so much packing to do!"

"Hold your horses," he smiled and made calming motions with his hands. "You have a few days yet. Listen can you get a baby-sitter for tonight? I'd like to take you out somewhere smart and then I can give you all the details."

Helena knew Madam Dzo was always happy to look after the children but she hesitated, not wanting to seem too eager and unused to receiving invitations now. After a few moments though she replied, "I think I could manage that. What time would suit you?"

They agreed that James would call by in a couple of hours and both parted, both with a feeling of 'Déjà vu' from when they had briefly been lovers in Chongqing.

At home Helena made the arrangements with her landlady, gave the children their simple supper and began to get ready. She still had one or two smart dresses to choose from that hadn't been worn for quite a while, for she always wore simple washable clothes to work. As she dressed she wondered where they would go; there were very few hotels or restaurants as far as she knew for Xian was not like Peking or indeed Shanghai where international communities thrived.

James arrived promptly as usual and handed Helena into the jeep with old-world courtesy. He gunned the motor and they set off with a roar.

"Where are we going?" asked Helena, as she noted they were heading away from the city centre.

"There's a place some of the guys told me about, near the Drum Tower – good food and a pretty view, so I'm told."

"Oh yes I saw some photos of the Drum Tower and the other one, the Bell Tower, that Erica took. It did look very picturesque. I haven't actually ventured to that part in all the time we've been here."

"I'm really hoping we'll have an evening to remember," smiled James, reaching over to put Helena's hand.

The first part of the evening went very well: the food was good, with spicy and robust flavours, and the ambience was comfortable. They chatted easily, mostly about the time in Chongqing but deliberately keeping the atmosphere light.

When the pot of jasmine tea had been filled for the third time, they sat back and James produced an envelope containing the 'tickets' for the plane that Helena and the children would take to Formosa. They were really just a scrap of paper with U.S. military stamps on.

"The flight goes in three days' time," explained James. "There's not much space, so I'm afraid you can only take one case each. Don't forget to bring your passports – not so much for this end but for when you land."

Helena's heart jumped into her mouth. "I haven't got my passport!" she cried.

"I thought you have a German passport from the embassy in Chongqing?" asked James.

"No! Don't you remember, the embassy was bombed before I could collect it! What shall I do?"

For the moment Helena was panic-stricken, having forgotten all about the need for papers.

James thought for a moment, then said "And what about the children? I guess they have no papers either?"

Helena shook her head and was near to tears.

"Don't worry," said James, taking her hand across the table. "I'm sure I can sort something out, even though it'll only be temporary travel passes at such short notice. Give me the details of all your full names and dates of birth."

Taking out a pen he proceeded to record all the details needed in a calm manner but the worry of this had spoilt the evening for Helena and she soon asked to go home to begin her packing.

As they parted at the door of the house, James explained that a courier would bring the papers and take them to the airstrip. He could not be certain about the time. "So be ready at any time on Thursday, ok?"

"Yes, we will. And thank you James. Thank you for everything. I don't know what I'd have done without your help."

James took he hand for a moment and said, "Be happy, Helena and be safe. Good bye." He turned away and did not look back. The evening had not quite been the romantic rendezvous he had envisaged, but, all in all, he was glad to have helped.

As Helena climbed the stairs she wiped away a few tears, remembering what they had been to each other. More pressing, however, was the anxiety about packing up her life in China and the trip itself. Her trusty baby-sitter had put the children to bed and was calmly waiting with a fresh pot of tea.

No better time than the present to explain her plans to her landlady, so Helena accepted a cup of tea and told her all the news. Madam Dzo was never surprised by anything but she did say that she would miss the little family.

"I must start packing, I've only got three days," said Helena, getting up and starting to open drawers and cupboards.

"It's late my dear, and you'll wake the children. Better to leave it until the morning."

Seeing the sense in this, they said Goodnight and Helena got ready for bed, not expecting to get much sleep. In fact, she slept quite quickly but only to be haunted by dreams in which her forthcoming journey to Free China was muddled up with all her other travels since she left Germany.

In the morning Helena thought it best to first explain the plan to the children and try to make it seem like an adventure, while hiding her anxiety about it all. Manfred and Chun seemed to accept the news quite readily and Manfred, in particular, offered to help by packing his own bag.

By late afternoon Helena had finished sorting out what to take and what to pass on to some of her school colleagues and Madam Dzo. She had also strengthened the fabric of her home-made money belt using some strong material from an old handbag. She would hide all of the gold she still had on her body for the journey – it would definitely be the safest way.

Manfred, too, had proudly finished packing his suitcase but his mother was not pleased when she found he had included most of his toys but no books.

"Take those toys out of there at once. We can only take important things like your school books." The stress of the move was getting to her and making her sharper than normal. Manfred didn't argue – he knew it wouldn't do any good – but the result of putting in so many books was that the case was really heavy – too heavy for the boy to lift so it was dragged to the door.

On the appointed day, quite early in the morning, a jeep drew up and the Marine hooted the horn. In a flurry of nerves and anxiety Helena began to get the children and the luggage downstairs, stopping only to hug Madam Dzo one last time. Seeing the bewilderment on the children's faces and the struggle the young woman was having, the soldier gave a hand and they were soon installed in the vehicle and on their way.

As soon as they set off Helena asked, "Do you have some papers for us? Lieutenant Baker said he would do that."

"Yes Ma'am. He said to tell you that they will be readily accepted by the U.S. authorities at the airport but you may need to explain about your husband's background to the Formosa officials."

"Oh, thank you," replied Helena, glad that she had carefully kept some of Fu Yan's certificates and commendations.

The plane was already on the runway and strong hands took care of the luggage and helped all three into the body of the aircraft. There were already a number of passengers installed on the makeshift seats but they managed to squeeze together on a sort of bench. Manfred wanted to look out but it was impossible to see anything from where they sat.

As they taxied along the runway and prepared for take-off the noise of the engines became deafening and Helena was terrified, holding the children close to her. Once in the air it didn't seem so bad and Manfred immediately began to ask questions along the lines of "When will we be there?" She couldn't answer that and in any case before long her daughter began to cry pathetically because her ears were hurting in the pressurised craft. Helena tried to comfort her but without success – she cried the whole flight. By the time the plane began to lose height for landing Helena was deeply concerned.

At last they landed with a grinding bump and the sigh of relief from everyone was audible. Chun was still snivelling as they disembarked and at this end there was no-one to help with the luggage. Everyone gathered up their belongings as best they could and made their way to the temporary building where the Taipei authorities were examining their papers. Helena and the children were way back in the queue and it looked like a long wait. Both children were very tired and Helena was really hot because she'd had to put on a thick padded jacket to hide the fact that she carried their gold around her body.

Slowly, slowly, they inched forward to the desk of the single official who was checking and questioning everyone. Helena was clutching the papers from the American office in Xian and the evidence she had of their background but her heart was still in her mouth – what if they sent them back? She was next in turn when there was suddenly a small commotion by the door and looking across she saw Gerda's husband waving to them while showing identification to a guard.

In moments he and another young man presumably an attaché, was at their side and ushering them around the desk and out into the fresh air.

Helena almost fainted with relief but she managed to thank her saviours.

"Thank you so much. How did you know we were here?"

"Well, there are only two planes a week so it wasn't too hard to check on each one. Come on you all look exhausted – let's get you home to Gerda."

They all piled into the embassy vehicle with the luggage and started back to the city. Helena closed her eyes and felt the relief wash over her. In a few moments, however, Manfred was excitedly shaking her to show her a large contingent of troops and tanks on a nearby field. She wondered briefly why there were so many but she didn't have the energy to enquire or even to engage in small talk at the moment.

After a drive of nearly an hour over some poorly made roads, they entered the city of Taipei and were soon drawing up outside an elegant villa-styled house that she recognised from the photos Gerda had sent. The car had barely stopped when the front door of the house flew open and out ran her dear friend.

Chapter 26

For the first few days Helena enjoyed being spoilt; the children could roam free in Gerda's large garden, the servants prepared delicious food and her friend insisted that she take enough time to recuperate from all the stress she had been under. In the evenings, when the children were in bed and the house quite calm, the two friends relaxed together, talking over old times and sharing tales of recent events in both of their lives. Gerda was mildly shocked to hear the full story of Erica's secret marriage and affair with Martin and admitted to feeling relieved that her own boys, though growing up, both seemed level headed.

"I know," replied Helena, "I sometimes think we spoilt her when she was young and since then she's always thought the plums should fall into her lap."

"Yes, she's beautiful and strong minded and that can be a fatal combination."

"Fatal for the men she meets, you mean?"

"Mmm, probably."

The two ladies fell silent for a while, sipping some sweet wine that a colleague of Gerda's husband had given them.

"This wine is delicious." remarked Helena. "You're so lucky to be able to get so many foreign things here."

"Yes. Well there are so many Americans here and you know how they like to make sure they have the best!"

After another short silence, Gerda began to drop hints that many local people were wanting to learn some English or improve their English to be able to deal with the Americans.

"I'm not asking you to think about leaving us, you're welcome to stay as long as you like, but maybe it would be a way for you to become independent by giving some private lessons."

"I could try that," replied Helena. "I certainly need to do something to support myself and the children because my gold won't last for ever."

"I'm sure something will work out, my dear." Gerda patted her friend's hand and they prepared to retire for the night, hopefully on a positive note.

The very next day a letter arrived for Helena that put any plans for the future onto a back burner for a while.

Dearest Mama,

Well so much has happened since we parted in Xian that I hardly know where to begin. I am hoping and praying that by now you and the kids are safe in Formosa with Gerda and her family. Oh dear, there is so much American influence here that I've started to use American words (kids).

When I arrived here I met up with some American girls and we have become good friends. I met them in the hotel where I was staying – it was really lovely there, elegant furnishings and delicious food, but Martin persuaded me that it was too expensive to stay for very long; I suppose he was right.

Martin was already working for an American newspaper and he too had made some friends. We've been invited to quite a few parties and outings. Yes, I guess we're a couple. We live in the same house but, don't worry, we have separate rooms.

Unfortunately I had no luck in finding a job. I took my portfolio of photos to every magazine we could think of but without success. Everyone says my work is really good so I'm not giving up yet.

The trouble is now, that Martin's paper has had to cease publication. People say it is because the owner of the paper was too critical of the new Chinese regime and he's disappeared. Some of the Chinese, especially young supporters of Mao, are quite anti-American and some of the girls I know don't like to go out in some parts of the city. Last week we heard that some American ladies were verbally abused near the embassy and I didn't really think anything of it until next day on the way home two young men deliberately bumped into me and called me a vile name; I felt really intimidated and ran to our house. When I told Martin he said not to go out alone any more, but I can't do that. He feels it happened because I'm Eurasian – maybe that's true.

Oh dear it sounds as though we are having an awful time here, which is not true and the really good news is that Martin has been asked to join a paper that is now based in Hong Kong. We have booked a passage for next month and we're really looking forward to it. I believe the lifestyle in Hong Kong will really suit us.

Martin has asked me to marry him. What do you think? Write to me with all your news as soon as you can.

Love to you and the little one's
Erica

Helena had taken the letter into the garden to read it and Gerda, peeping out, saw that she was sitting with her head bowed and tears in her eyes.

"What's the matter Helena? Is it bad news?

She didn't answer, just passed over the letter. Gerda sat down, read the letter and looking up, saw that Helena had dried her eyes.

"That's all ok," Gerda said, taking her friends' hand. "At least Hong Kong is safe, probably safer than here."

"What do you mean Gerda?"

"Well you can see what she's said about the trouble between Americans and the Chinese regime – it's the reason for most of the American presence here. The U.S. Army is training up Nationalist Chinese to help defend the island. My husband says it maybe just 'sabre rattling' but you never know."

"Oh, I remember we saw lots of military vehicles on the way here. Manfred was very interested in them."

As she said this, Helena looked across to where the children were playing a complicated three-way game of marbles with one of Gerda's sons. Was there to be a future for them here in Formosa or not?"

"You better write back straight away so she gets it before they sail. What are you going to say about the marriage?"

"Makes no difference what I say. She'll do whatever she wants!"

Gerda nodded and got up to leave "Come and help me in the kitchen when you've done – I'm organising a little supper party. There's a really nice chap I'd like you to meet."

Chapter 27

Martin could not believe the amount of luggage that Erica packed up for the voyage to Hong Kong. He knew she had brought several bags and boxes when she arrived in Shanghai, but where had all the rest come from? When he tentatively asked her about it, he was at first told, in no uncertain terms, that it was none of his business but then she smiled that bewitching smile and explained, "I'll need to look my best in Hong Kong – there are lots of elegant women there and lots of elegant places to go. And, after we're married, I'm sure you'll want your wife to be well dressed."

Martin caught his breath at this; Erica had asked for time to consider his proposal which he'd finally, nervously stammered out several weeks ago and he'd almost given up hope of acceptance. He knew she was really out of his league, so beautiful and vivacious but she was now saying YES. He caught her in his arms and whirled her around in a most uncharacteristic way before kissing her sweetly and gently on the lips. That feeling of desire he'd fought so hard to control now would not be controlled and he longed to take her in his arms and make love to her.

Erica pushed him away though and, smiling coquettishly, said "Not now, I must finish the packing."

On board ship the conditions were very cramped, not helped by the mountain of luggage and both Erica and Martin began to feel queasy soon after leaving port. A friendly Chinese couple gave them ginger tea which helped a lot. It was useful talking to them as well because they had some relations on the island who had found digs for them in an area that seemed to be a good starting point.

Erica had wanted to stay in a hotel until they could find something permanent but Martin said they couldn't afford it at the moment. It wasn't in Erica's nature to sulk but when it came to it she simply refused to go a lodging house and went to a hotel instead.

There were three items on Martin's immediate agenda: settling into his new job, finding an apartment and contacting the priest, a past colleague, who had been instrumental in securing his post for him. These things took up most of his time but he still made sure to meet Erica each day, when they would talk and make plans for their wedding. Much to Martin's surprise Erica wanted only a very low-key affair and insisted that they be married before she moved into an apartment with him.

It didn't take long for Martin and Erica to start making new friends. Erica had immediately purchased more film for her camera and set about adding to her portfolio of art photographs thinking that she could contrast the culture of China with Hong Kong – old to new or East to West. Her naturally gregarious nature and sunny personality shone from behind the camera and led her into many conversations and some potential friendships.

The island itself was buzzing with growth; everywhere building was going on to accommodate the thousands of new arrivals from

China. Homes and access roads were appearing at amazing speed in and around the expanding city. Work on the many projects went on day and night so that, when the temperature was warm enough to necessitate keeping windows open at night, sleep was often disturbed by the blasting, drilling and hammering.

The whole island was bursting with life and Erica found herself almost spoilt for choice as to subjects for her camera: there was the beautiful Botanic Garden, the bustling harbour and crowded markets to name but a few. Her acquisitive nature led her also to the smart department stores where she admired the latest American fashions. Searching through a rack of light cotton dresses, she suddenly heard her named called and turned to see Mary Lou, one of the first friends she had made in Shanghai.

"Mary Lou, how great to see you!"

"And you, my dear! What a small world it's become. How are you and how's that delicious fiancé of yours?"

Mary Lou linked her arm through Erica's saying, "Come on you must tell me all your news. There's a great place just down the road where they do real American sodas and milkshakes."

The café was fairly busy but cool and they found a quiet corner table where they could catch up.

The first thing Mary Lou said, checking out her friend's left hand, was, "I thought you would be married by now – you haven't changed your mind have you?"

"Oh no, I think we'll get married in a few weeks when Martin has found an apartment. It would be lovely if you and Chuck could be our witnesses."

"No way, I want to be your Matron of Honour!"

"We're only having a very quick ceremony, nothing like that," replied Erica.

Mary Lou was very surprised and couldn't help suspecting that they had some problems.

"Where is Martin? Is he working?"

Yes, he's busy everyday with something or other."

Erica sipped her cooling soda and looked across at her companion saying, "You know I can't believe we've just bumped into each other like this, it's such a coincidence."

"Not really," replied Mary Lou, "since all the restrictions of the Communist regime have started to bite, half of Shanghai is here and sometimes it seems like half of China as well. Everywhere is so packed and, well, you've seen all the building that going on."

"Yes it's much busier than I expected but I do like it here, don't you? It's certainly got a buzz to it and the shopping is great!"

"Oh sure – I'm glad we came here, rather than going to Formosa where we had another opportunity. Chuck reckons there's a real danger that Mao might try to invade Free China as they call it."

Mary Lou checked her watch and got ready to rush off to another appointment but not before making arrangements to meet Erica and Martin for cocktails the following evening.

Erica sat a while digesting that last piece of news. To Mary Lou it had seemed almost a throwaway line but it had a worrying significance to her.

Martin was reluctant to meet the Americans for cocktails, suspecting it would mean a long interrogation about his past, but agreed to go because he knew Erica loved that kind of thing. She dressed in a smart cocktail suit of silver and black that he hadn't seen before and he had to admit that she looked stunning. Any man would feel proud, he thought, to walk down the street with her and indeed several heads turned but not really for the reasons he thought.

The atmosphere and décor in the small cocktail bar was cool and elegant to the point of opulence. Martin's immediate concern was that the drinks would be extremely expensive. Mary Lou and her husband Chuck were already seated at a table with another couple who turned out to be British government staff. Polite small talk gradually merged into more serious topics and, although the conversation was general, Martin had the uncomfortable feeling that he was being judged.

After several rounds of cocktails someone suggested they go on down to Aberdeen to dine and the group surged out onto the busy street. Martin hung back and caught Erica's hand saying quietly, "I don't think we ought to go with them – tell them we had another appointment."

"I will not!" hissed Erica. "Don't be such a bore, come on, it'll be fun!"

The restaurant boats were busy as always but they managed to secure a table and before long were enjoying super-fresh seafood and crisp vegetables. The ambience here was much more casual and informal than the bar had been and everyone relaxed and enjoyed the rest of the evening. On leaving to get back to shore, however, Erica overheard the British woman, Ivy, remark "Well she's done well for herself, hasn't she! Hmm. The Eurasian girl and the missionary – sounds like an X-rated movie." Peals of laughter followed this cruel remark.

She might have known that the apartment Martin found would be a dump – and it was! He was so excited about it that he paid a deposit and a month's rent before she even saw it.

"Well, I suppose we can brighten it up a bit with some curtains and things," Erica said uncertainly.

She knew she'd no choice really because the hotel was clamouring for their bill to be paid and also they could now get married and put a stop to the gossip about them. Mary Lou had explained that a lot of Hong Kong society found mixed race relationships unacceptable and could make things difficult. They had never come across such prejudice in Shanghai or anywhere else for that matter.

Martin and Erica had a long heart to heart about it. In his usual calm way he dismissed such narrow-minded attitudes as ignorance and thoroughly convinced her that anyone who thought like that wasn't worth knowing anyway.

"There's something else bothering you as well though, isn't there. You've not been yourself for a while now."

Erica nodded and began to tell him about her mother and the children, following what Mary Lou had said about the instability in Formosa. She hadn't worried too much about us until, in her mother's recent letter, there had been mention of the high American presence together with a childish drawing of a tank from Manfred.

Martin gathered her into his arms in a rare show of physical affection and whispered, "Oh my darling, you are such a tender-hearted girl. Don't worry there will always be a place for them with us if they need it."

He kissed her as if to seal the promise and then said, "Come on now, let's get ready to go out. There's a bridge party at the Peninsula and I'm required!"

Martin's skill at bridge had earned them many invitations and new acquaintances for he was a mean player and often in demand. Erica didn't play bridge but was happy to go along as it meant excuses to dress up and drink cocktails.

If Martin had hoped that marriage would convert Erica into a homely housewife he was sadly mistaken. Certainly she did use her artistic talents to furnish and decorate the apartment most attractively and she could produce tasty and nourishing meals if she felt like it but the humdrum aspects of laundry, cleaning and marketing bored her. More and more often they were obliged to eat out as there was little in the larder. While eating out in Hong Kong was pleasant and not too expensive, it was obviously more expensive than home cooking.

Erica's extravagance began to cause rows between them, the biggest when she announced she wanted to engage a servant to do the cleaning and cooking.

"Mary Lou says it doesn't cost much. She has one and so do all her friends so I think we should too."

"No, Erica, we can't afford it."

Chapter 28

As usual Gerda's 'little supper party' turned out to be a beautiful evening buffet for over thirty people. Always the perfect hostess she made sure to introduce Helena to two or three of the early comers so she wasn't awkwardly alone for a moment. The guests were a cosmopolitan mix of mostly Chinese and Americans but a sprinkling of other nationalities to add spice. Everyone was very friendly and quick with offers of helpful advice when they learnt that Helena and the children were recently arrived from China.

A little later Helena began to realise she was feeling a little light-headed due to drinking Champagne on an empty stomach. She felt very hungry, having not eaten much all day, so she excused herself to collect some food from the buffet. The table was still laden with delicious salads and a mixture of European style canapes as well as dim sum. Helena had only eaten a few mouthfuls when Gerda appeared at her side saying, "Oh my dear, do come and meet my good friend Leon."

She whisked her across the room to where a smartly dressed Chinese man had just entered. He was quite short with delicate features, smooth skin and kind eyes. To Helena's surprise, as they were introduced, he spoke to her in fluent German.

"Oh, you speak German. How wonderful!"

"Yes, I have studied and lived in Germany for some years. Before the war I spent some very happy times there."

Gerda quietly disappeared, leaving the two to get to know each other, aware that they had a lot in common.

Leon had studied in Hanover but had visited Berlin several times so they reminisced about some of the sights and landmarks. He, too, had married a German girl before returning to Shanghai but she had sadly died after the birth of their third child.

Although Leon and Helena had only just met they found themselves sharing confidences as though they were old friends. After a time Leon suggested he fetch them both a glass of Champagne and as he walked over to the serving area Helena found herself thinking how glad she was that she'd made time to wash her hair that afternoon and put on a little lipstick. When he returned with the drinks, they moved outside and sat on a bench in the garden where Gerda's boys had hung coloured lanterns in the trees. Helena would come to remember that evening as the first time in years that she'd felt at peace.

All too soon the guests began to leave and Leon got up to go.

"Good bye," said Helena, "it's been really nice talking to you."

"I wonder if you would allow me to take you to dinner tomorrow?" asked Leon, taking her hand for a moment.

"Oh that would be lovely, thank you."

"Wonderful. Shall I call for you at seven?"

Helena nodded and walked with him to the door. As she closed the door after him Gerda appeared out of nowhere with a big smile on her face.

"I knew you two would get on well – he's lovely, isn't he?"

"He's very nice," replied Helena, trying not to smile too much while realising that inside she felt like a girl on her first date.

Next morning Helena woke with a throbbing head courtesy of too much Champagne and reality quickly kicked in. There was no time for day-dreaming she had to start finding somewhere to live, sort out schools and advertise for some students. Before she was even dressed though, Chun came into her room crying that Manfred had been mean to her and had gone out with his air-gun. Helena gave her daughter a quick cuddle and tried to pacify her but this bought to her mind again how the girl was becoming so clingy while Manfred was getting out of control.

After breakfast she set off into the city with Gerda and they were very lucky to quickly find a small furnished apartment vacant in a modern building. Without hesitation they made arrangements to take over the lease at the end of the week.

"Oh, thanks for your help Gerda, that's such a relief now perhaps I can start to get the children settled again. Is there a school for them near here?"

"I don't know but we needn't worry about that today – we have a more pressing mission. You need a new dress for your date tonight!"

Helena didn't need much persuading and the two headed to a large store where they could find American off-the-peg dresses. Both remembered the times way back in Peking when dresses were specially made for them but it was perhaps even more fun to be able to try dresses on straight away. Helena chose a pale green silky frock with a deep V-neck, nipped in waist and a full skirt as well as a polka-dot sun dress and they headed home very satisfied with the day.

Seeing her mother getting ready to go out, Chun started to whine and fuss so much that Helena thought perhaps she shouldn't go.

"Don't be ridiculous! Of course you must go." Gerda took charge and whisked the snivelling child off to the kitchen for milk and cookies.

Leon arrived promptly and immediately complimented her on the new dress. The car parked at the kerb was an almost-new Mercedes – very impressive. Helena didn't say anything as he opened the door for her but as she settled into the sumptuous seat she felt things were all coming right.

For dinner Leon had chosen a small restaurant on the outskirts of the city, suggesting that the larger ones in the centre became quite noisy so that it's hard to talk. Helena agreed she was quite happy with that and settled back to enjoy the evening.

The restaurant was indeed small and quite intimate; the food was simple but well cooked. During dinner Helena learnt that Leon's children, three of them, were in America with his wife's sister, having been sent there for safety and to get a better education.

"Don't you miss them awfully though?" she asked.

"No not really – we can keep in touch by letter and I know they're actually better off there while things are unsettled in China."

Helena was thoughtful for a few moments but she didn't want to spoil the evening so they then fell to chatting about her imminent move away from Gerda's house. As she had hoped Leon quickly offered any help they might need in moving or getting settled.

"Thank you so much – you are such a kind man."

I hope you will think of me as a good friend, Helena." Leon smiled and laid his hand over hers.

After dinner the evening was still pleasant, with just a soft balmy breeze so Leon suggested a stroll to the nearby Confucian Temple.

As they entered the beautiful exotic portals the peace inside seemed to envelop them. It was dark by now but the moonlight was strong enough to illuminate the gardens and walk-ways. Evening scented flowers like jasmine and hibiscus gave off their perfume enhancing the romantic atmosphere. Strolling in the moonlight it seemed so natural to hold hands and to stop for a gentle kiss.

The move was painlessly accomplished – well after all they hadn't brought much with them from China. Sometimes Helena couldn't help thinking of all the things they'd left behind on their various moves, fleeing from both the Japanese and the Communists. No point in dwelling on that though – what's past is past.

Leon had been so helpful in piling all their belongings and the children into the car for the short journey. Manfred, of course, was most impressed by the car.

A few days later Gerda invited herself to tea, ostensibly to see how they were settling in but really to find out how her 'matchmaking' with Leon was going.

"I can see you've settled quite well but then you're used to moving aren't you. How are the children? Are they out?"

"Chun's at home – she's playing with her dolls in her room but Manfred's out. He never wants to stay home and he never wants to study and he takes no notice of what I say."

"Yes it's difficult when they get older – boys especially, I think."

"I'm really worried about their future, you know. Did you know that Leon sent his children to their aunt in America for safety and a good education. I wish I knew someone in America but I don't."

"No, but you know someone in Hong Kong and someone who has contacts in Ireland and England – if they could go to school in England, that would be ideal."

"Do you know I hadn't thought of that but it's a possibility, isn't it?"

"I think it's the ideal solution. Why don't you sound out Erica next time you write?"

"Yes I might just do that – it's certainly something to think about."

"Mmm, now come on," said Gerda, settling back in her chair, "tell me about you and Leon."

"There's nothing to tell. I've seen him a few times, we're friends and he's a very nice man."

"Well don't forget I'll always have the children if you want to go out."

"Thank you and thanks for giving me that idea. You're such a good friend and it always helps to talk to you."

"We aim to please," smiled Gerda airily as she got up to leave.

As they parted on the doorstep, Leon's car drew up and he got out.

"Oh here's Leon," said Gerda. "Were you expecting him?"

"No, not at all," replied Helena. "Do I look alright?"

"You look perfect, my dear, but what does it matter? He's just a very nice man!" With a smile and a huge wink she tripped down the path, greeting Leon on the way.

Leon had brought house-warming gifts in the form of a lovely bunch of flowers and some good German wine.

"Oh, that's so kind of you, thank you," smiled Helena as she stood aside to welcome him in and closed the door.

"We must drink some wine straight away to warm the house."

"Good idea," replied Leon, taking the chair that she indicated.

While Helena was in the kitchen collecting glasses and a few nuts to accompany the wine, Leon opened the bottle and looking around, noting how she had made the place quite homely in just a few days.

Raising their glasses Helena toasted, "Prosit," but Leon's words were "To the future!"

After one small glass of wine, Leon rose saying he had only called in for a short time but asked if she would be free at the weekend.

"I would love to show you around the island, there are some very beautiful places."

Helena hesitated, thinking she would have to make arrangements for the children but then remembered that Gerda had offered just a short time ago.

"That would be really nice – thank you so much."

Leon picked her up before lunch. It was a beautiful day, clear skies but not too hot; the children had been happy to go to Gerda's, knowing they could play in her large garden. Helena wore the new sun dress matched with white shoes and bag borrowed from Gerda. She felt like a young girl again, freed from her responsibilities for a while.

They drove to the coast where Leon knew a small seafood restaurant, chatting as they travelled about anything and everything – he was so easy to talk to. Over a lunch of delicious soft-shelled crabs they talked a bit about Helena's tentative plan to arrange the children's education abroad. Leon didn't say too much but agreed that they might well be safer away from Formosa.

After lunch and back in the car they took a scenic trip along the coast and finally to the famous Hot Springs at Beitou. Here Leon took her hand as they walked beside the hot streams, along terraces beneath shady trees. The atmosphere was idyllically peaceful and so pretty with lots of little bridges crossing and re-crossing the water that supplied the old Japanese Boathouse, a building rather like Roman baths. The flowing water and dense greenery was so calming that they sat for a while on a rustic bench in thoughtful silence – most unusual for them.

At last Leon turned to Helena, took her hand between his and almost whispered, "I suppose you know I'm very much in love with you. Maybe you think it is too soon but I want to ask you to marry me."

She was surprised, they'd barely known each other for three weeks and although she was fond of him, this felt like a bolt out of the blue.

Helena just stared at him for a few moments, then smiled.

"I'll understand if you need some time to think about it. Do you?"

She just nodded and then couldn't say anything anyway because he was kissing her with a passion that startled her. After a short time they continued on their walk, hand in hand; she still hadn't said anything at all.

Getting back to the car some time later he courteously handed her into the seat, got in beside her and looked across questioningly.

Helena took a deep breath. "Yes I will marry you but on one condition – no more children."

Leon burst out laughing, "That's fine by me." Then, looking absolutely delighted, he produced a tiny ring box containing the biggest diamond she had ever seen.

Chapter 29

"Hi, Honey! Guess what!"

What a pleasant change it was for Martin to have a warm smiling greeting after the day's work. Too often lately his wife had been despondent and cool, not really fitting into the Hong Kong society as she had expected. None of the magazines she had tried showed much interest in her photography and she found her daily chores 'too tedious for words'.

Whatever had caused this outburst, he was delighted.

"I can't guess." He laughed, gathering her into his arms. "Come on tell me."

"Well, I've had a letter from Mama and, "she paused for effect, "she's getting married! Not only that, he's a Chinese guy from Shanghai and like Vati he studied in Germany so he speaks fluent German. Isn't that marvellous?"

"That really is good news. I'm so pleased for her, she deserves some happiness after all she's been through. But does that make a difference to her plans for the children?"

"No, I don't think so – I'll ask when I write back and I'll need to get all the details. She said they hope to arrange the wedding quite soon and we'll obviously need to be there."

Martin sat down and sighed. "I don't think that's possible; I can't get time off just like that and anyway you know we can't afford such a trip."

"But we have to! How often does your mother get married? You can stay if you want but I'm going. I'll find a way."

So saying, she swept off into their tiny kitchen and began chopping vegetables noisily and rattling a wok.

Martin remained in the living room, reading his newspaper, knowing there was no point in arguing with her. The good humour hadn't lasted very long but much as he would like to promise her the moon he really couldn't at the moment.

After supper they generally cleared up together and then went out for a stroll, often ending up in a club for a cocktail or in a waterfront café for a pot of tea but tonight Erica said she was going to write back to Mama straight away so Martin was left to go alone.

"That's fine," he said "I won't be long, please send my congratulations too. Also could you tell your mother that I've made some enquiries and it seems that the best plan for the children's education would be for us to legally adopt them so that they could get British Passports."

"Oh, thanks for checking that out. We'll have to see what they want to do now."

Martin smiled, kissed her proffered cheek lightly and went out for his walk. It was a balmy evening and he always enjoyed the sight and smells of the city. Wandering through the market, the buzz of trade and banter was enervating as he was greeted by several of the stall holders whom they had got to know. Soon he turned back towards home feeling relaxed and confident.

﹡

Helena opened the letter from Erica with some trepidation, hoping the news of her forthcoming wedding would be greeted with more enthusiasm than the younger children had shown; they didn't dislike Leon but Manfred would have preferred a soldier and Chan wished he was a prince! The content both cheered and saddened her and after reading it twice she folded it and put it in her bag to show Leon when they met later.

Their appointment was in a small café near to Leon's office where they would have a cup of tea during his lunch time break. When Leon arrived she was already seated at their usual table deeply absorbed in re-reading the letter. Looking up as he sat down, she smiled but not very convincingly.

"Is something wrong?" he asked, taking her hand.

"No, not really," she replied. "I've had a long letter from Erica – there's good news and bad news. Here, see what you think."

Leon took the letter, read it carefully and thoroughly, then calmly folded it and looked up at his fiancée.

"Well," he said, "you'd better write back and say we will send her a ticket because she must come for the wedding – I know you'd like that wouldn't you!"

Helena gasped and hugged him but before she could say anything he continued, "I also think Martin's suggestion about the children is very sensible and I think they'll need some help with the expenses for that as well."

By now Helena had tears in her eyes. "Oh Leon, thank you so much – you are so good to me."

❋

Erica arrived almost two weeks before the date set for the wedding, bearing gifts for the children and for the groom as well as enough luggage for quite a long visit. The children were delighted to see their big sister, knowing that there was always fun and laughter when she was around. Leon had gone with Helena to meet her daughter from the ferry, taking a lovely bunch of carnations as a welcome gift. It was a real pleasure to Helena that Erica and Leon seem to hit it off right away.

Next evening they were all invited to supper by Gerda and they all had a lovely evening. By the time they were enjoying the dessert of German-style plum cake, Erica and Leon were laughing and joking as though they'd known each other for years.

The wedding plans were well underway. The official ceremony would take place in a government office with just two witnesses present, Gerda and Erica, then the party would adjourn to a nearby hotel for the reception. Leon had booked a private room in the Plum Garden Hotel, deliberately chosen because of its good reputation and its proximity to the Hot Springs at Beitou where he had proposed – he could be very romantic.

A shopping spree was called for when mother and daughter shopped heroically as both needed wedding outfits and Helena needed a trousseau for the honeymoon in Singapore, also booked by Leon as a surprise treat.

The wedding day dawned bright and clear – it was going to be a perfect day. Gerda arrived early with Champagne and nibbles to enjoy while Helena got ready. Gerda's family were going to take Manfred and Chun direct to the party at the hotel so they had a couple of hours to just enjoy getting ready. Erica was already busy clicking away with her camera to record every aspect of the day.

Right on time the taxi arrived to take them to the ceremony. Helena wore a cream suit trimmed with navy and matching navy shoes. She carried a gorgeous spray of cerise Singapore orchids. Erica had thought the outfit was perhaps a bit too formal and severe but had to agree that the bride had a glow from within that lifted the simple costume to the level of couture. Leon obviously thought the same as he met them at the door of the chamber, beaming with pride and joy.

Helena had been past the Plum Garden Hotel but never inside, so she was thrilled and delighted at its pleasant atmosphere. The reception and public areas had just the right mix of comfort, luxury and tranquillity. All the guests were gathered in the main lounge enjoying a drink when the newlyweds arrived to cheers and claps. The room where the buffet was set out opened onto a spacious veranda and the hotel's elegant gardens.

There was a wonderful array of finger foods, a beautiful cake and plenty of Champagne.

Erica of course, had appointed herself official photographer and used her skills in taking both formal posed pictures as well as charming candid shots of bride and groom as well as the guests.

All in all, the whole day was perfect.

Chapter 30

Erica stayed in Formosa while her parents were away in Singapore. She looked after the children (with help from Gerda) and busied herself putting together an album of memories from the wedding. Gerda's husband agreed to let her use the office telephone so she could phone Martin to compare thoughts the adults had about the children's future.

The plan was that Manfred and Chun should go back to Hong Kong with their sister and stay with Erica and Martin, learning English, until their adoption and passports could be completed. The general consensus seemed to be that this could take up to a year. Then Manfred was to be sent to a boarding school in England, run by the Christian Order that Martin had belonged to; a bit later Chun was to go to a convent school in Ireland near to Martin's family. Any objections from the children were dismissed as it was deemed best for their future and it was presented to them as a great adventure.

When Helena and Leon returned it was a matter of only a few weeks to pack and secure passages to Hong Kong.

During this time there was so much to do and arrange that Helena didn't have time to fret about the situation or about another potential bomb shell that life had thrown at them. As soon as they were back from Singapore Leon had learnt that his company was almost definitely relocating to Indonesia – such was the potential threat of Chinese communism.

He had told his wife this news quietly when they were alone and they agreed not to even think about it and what it might mean to their future until the children were safely in Hong Kong.

On the day of departure the children were, of course, excited and the adults made sure to keep cheerful faces although Helena, at least, was silently praying that they were doing the right thing. It wasn't until the ship pulled away with passengers and onlookers waving hard that she allowed herself a few tears.

Leon drove them straight back into town and they went to see a comedy film which always cheered Helena up. Afterwards they went to their favourite restaurant for a meal and deliberately kept conversation light for the rest of the day.

It was more than a week before either Helena or Leon mentioned the proposed move though it was definitely on both their minds. At last Leon bit the bullet and said, "Come and sit down my dear, we must decide what to do about the company and the move."

"Have we got any choice?" asked Helena.

"Well, yes, apparently the move would be to Djakarta, which is quite a pleasant city but I've been thinking it might be a good time for me to leave the company and start my own business."

"Could we afford that?"

"I'd get a good severance pay from the company so I think we could manage."

Helena thought for a moment and then took his hand, saying "Do you know, I'd really like that – I've been simply dreading another move."

"Oh, I don't mean stay here. I think we should move back to Germany. You'd like that wouldn't you?"

Helena couldn't believe her ears; she jumped up and hugged her husband. Tears came to her eyes as she whispered "I'd really love it. It would be going home."